STAR WARS

ATTACK OF THE CLONES

INCREDIBLE CROSS-SECTIONS

Written by
CURTIS SAXTON

Illustrated by
**HANS JENSSEN &
RICHARD CHASEMORE**

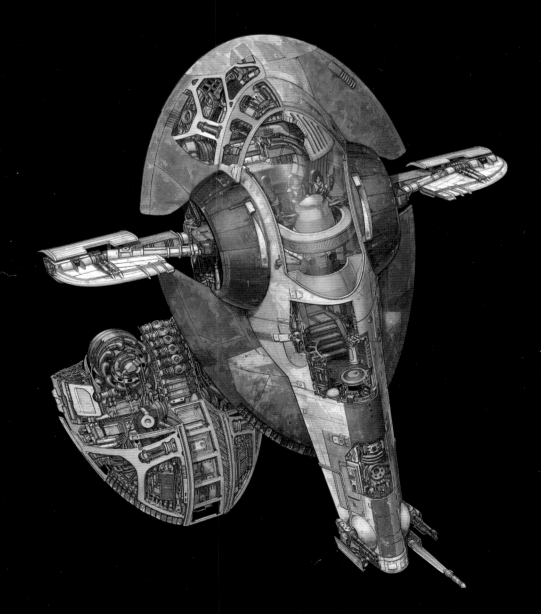

www.starwars.com

www.dk.com

CONTENTS

INTRODUCTION
3

NABOO CRUISER
4

ZAM'S AIRSPEEDER
6

ANAKIN'S AIRSPEEDER
8

JEDI STARFIGHTER
10

SLAVE I
12

OWEN LARS' SWOOP BIKE
14

PADMÉ'S STARSHIP
16

TRADE FEDERATION CORE SHIP
18

GEONOSIAN FIGHTER
20

REPUBLIC ASSAULT SHIP
22

REPUBLIC GUNSHIP
24

AT-TE
28

SOLAR SAILER
30

ACKNOWLEDGEMENTS
32

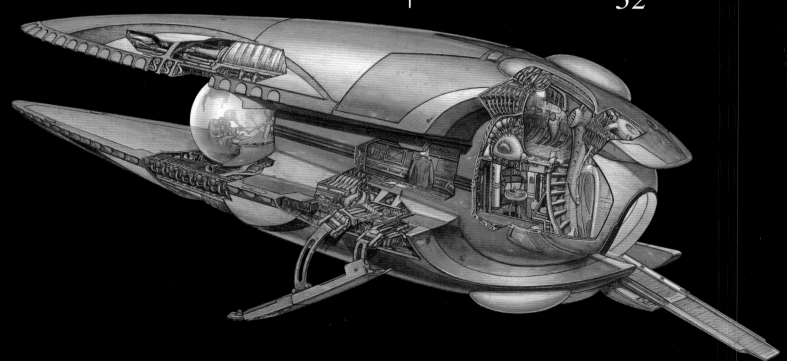

INTRODUCTION

IN OVER 25,000 YEARS since the exploitation of hyperdrive technology finally united the galaxy, the basic attributes of starflight have remained constant. Few now presume to question the quintillions of engineering pioneers active in the Early Hyperspace Age. Artistic expression and raw practicality have long been the sole ideals of vehicle design. However, as political deadlock and disfunction permeate the galaxy, peculiar mechanical forms are now beginning to merge. Greedy commercial organizations have burst from relative obscurity to challenge galactic law with their bizarrely melded, mercantile/military apparatus. In response, a mighty mechanized force, created in secret, is used for the first time to aid the Jedi in their guardianship of the disoriented but legitimate Galactic Republic. The tolerant diversity of millions of planetary cultures, expressed in countless local styles of starship design, is now being eroded by bitter secessionism as the cataclysmic Clone Wars begin.

TECHNOLOGY

ENERGY WEAPONS

Energy weapons fire invisible energy beams at lightspeed. The visible "bolt" is a glowing pulse that travels along the beam at less than lightspeed. Therefore, targets can explode instants before the "bolt" actually arrives. The light given off by visible bolts depletes the overall energy content of a beam, limiting its range. Turbolasers gain a longer range by spinning the energy beam, which reduces waste glow. A gun's range also depends on its aiming precision and the time-lag required to detect and anticipate target motion at a distance. For example, a massive warship mounts small point-defence guns that trade power for quick aim, while heavier guns are effective against slow, distant, large targets.

POWER SOURCES

Starships and vehicles use a hierarchy of power technologies that were perfected in pre-Republic ages. Low-power, domestic machines run on portable chemical, fission, and fusion reactors, which consume a variety of fuels depending on local resources. Most starships use fusion systems that confine more-powerful hypermatter annihilation cores. The interiors of the mightiest war vessels are dominated by huge reactor cores and ultra-dense fuel silos, which enable them to perform massive planetary bombardments and sustain hours of thousand-G accelerations before refuelling.

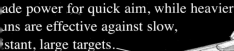

HYPERSPACE

Hyperdrives allow voyages through an eerie realm called hyperspace—i.e. the ordinary universe viewed from a ship travelling faster than the speed of light. Hyperdrives adjust faster-than-light "hypermatter" particles to allow a jump to light-speed without changing the complex mass and energy of the ship. In addition to hyperdrive travel, an equally wondrous technology exists, called hyperwaves: supralight signals for real-time transgalactic communications through public HoloNet relays. Hyperwave transceivers require almost stellar-scale power, yet signals can be blocked by nearby massive obstructions or by deflector shielding.

GRAVITY TECHNOLOGY

Modern galactic civilization manipulates gravity confidently. Gravity-altering devices include repulsorlifts that allow unpowered antigravity floatation, tractor-beam projectors for remote application of force, and acceleration compensators that prevent pulverization of starship occupants during maneuvers. The gravitoactive constituents of these devices are subnuclear knots of space-time made in enormous, unmanned power refineries encompassing black holes.

SHIELDS

Conventional shield technologies use a range of force-field effects. Ray shields, for example, deflect or break up energy beams, while particle shields forcefully retard high-velocity projectiles. Normally, shield intensities diminish gradually with distance from the generator or projector. However, shields projected in an atmosphere tend to have a defined outer surface. Such a boundary becomes super-hot when left still, and mirage-like effects are seen. Shields surrounding a moving airborne vessel are less visible, but can impact on aerodynamic performance. When a shield absorbs large energy blasts, the momentum can surge back to the ship and affect its motion. Shields do not operate without cost: Constant power is required to dissipate the energy from impacts.

NABOO CRUISER

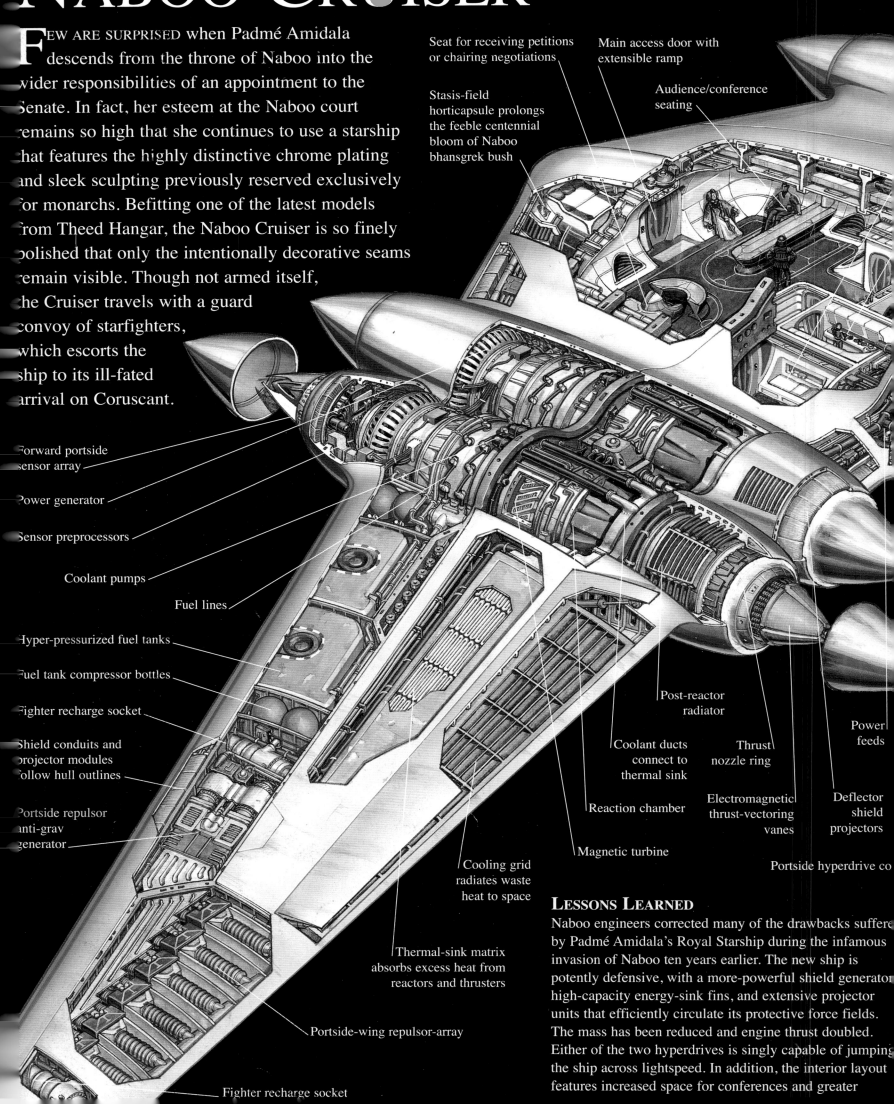

EW ARE SURPRISED when Padmé Amidala
descends from the throne of Naboo into the
wider responsibilities of an appointment to the
Senate. In fact, her esteem at the Naboo court
remains so high that she continues to use a starship
that features the highly distinctive chrome plating
and sleek sculpting previously reserved exclusively
for monarchs. Befitting one of the latest models
from Theed Hangar, the Naboo Cruiser is so finely
polished that only the intentionally decorative seams
remain visible. Though not armed itself,
the Cruiser travels with a guard
convoy of starfighters,
which escorts the
ship to its ill-fated
arrival on Coruscant.

Seat for receiving petitions
or chairing negotiations

Main access door with
extensible ramp

Audience/conference
seating

Stasis-field
horticapsule prolongs
the feeble centennial
bloom of Naboo
bhansgrek bush

Forward portside
sensor array

Power generator

Sensor preprocessors

Coolant pumps

Fuel lines

Hyper-pressurized fuel tanks

Fuel tank compressor bottles

Fighter recharge socket

Shield conduits and
projector modules
follow hull outlines

Portside repulsor
anti-grav
generator

Post-reactor
radiator

Coolant ducts
connect to
thermal sink

Thrust
nozzle ring

Power
feeds

Reaction chamber

Electromagnetic
thrust-vectoring
vanes

Deflector
shield
projectors

Magnetic turbine

Portside hyperdrive co

Cooling grid
radiates waste
heat to space

Thermal-sink matrix
absorbs excess heat from
reactors and thrusters

LESSONS LEARNED

Naboo engineers corrected many of the drawbacks suffere
by Padmé Amidala's Royal Starship during the infamous
invasion of Naboo ten years earlier. The new ship is
potently defensive, with a more-powerful shield generator
high-capacity energy-sink fins, and extensive projector
units that efficiently circulate its protective force fields.
The mass has been reduced and engine thrust doubled.
Either of the two hyperdrives is singly capable of jumping
the ship across lightspeed. In addition, the interior layout
features increased space for conferences and greater

Portside-wing repulsor-array

Fighter recharge socket

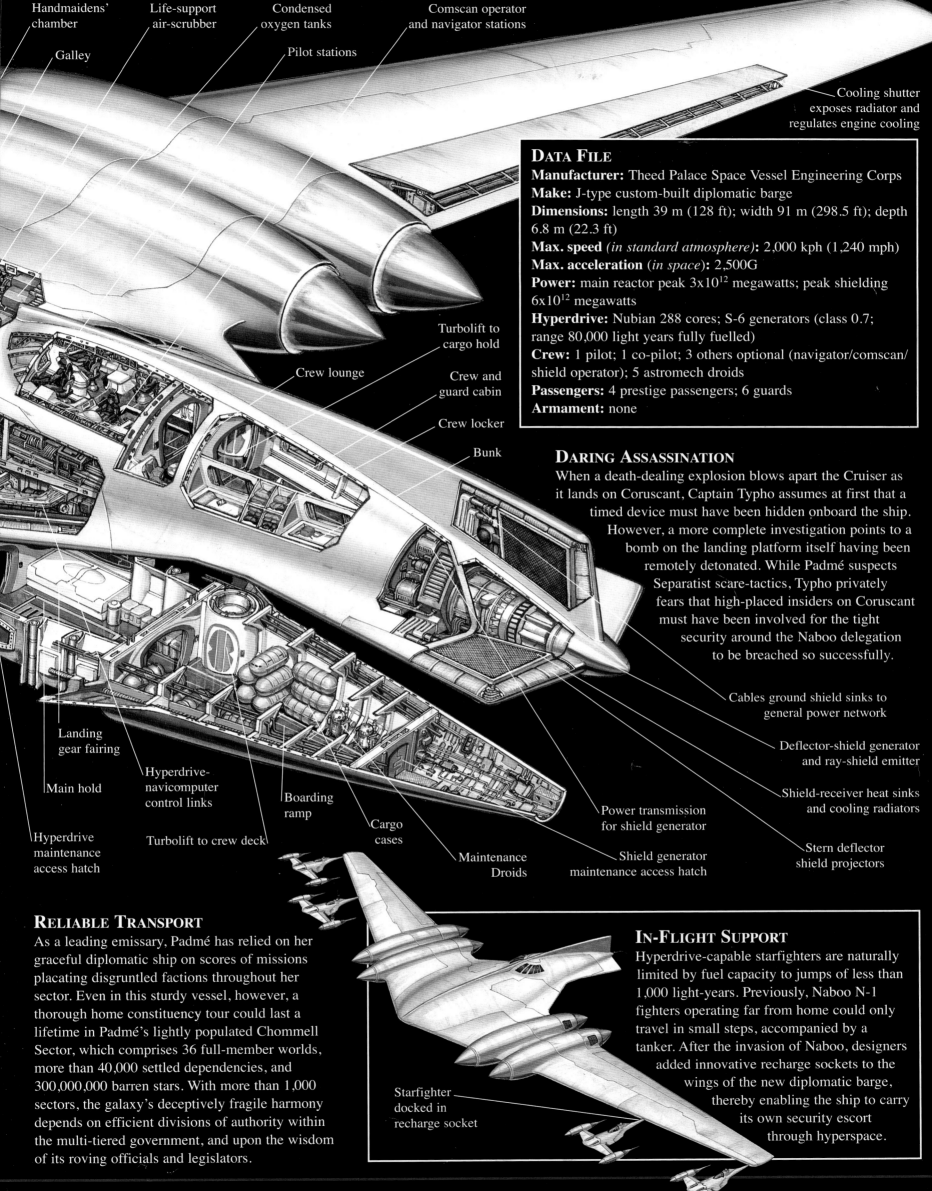

Handmaidens' chamber

Life-support air-scrubber

Condensed oxygen tanks

Comscan operator and navigator stations

Galley

Pilot stations

Cooling shutter exposes radiator and regulates engine cooling

Turbolift to cargo hold

Crew lounge

Crew and guard cabin

Crew locker

Bunk

DATA FILE

Manufacturer: Theed Palace Space Vessel Engineering Corps
Make: J-type custom-built diplomatic barge
Dimensions: length 39 m (128 ft); width 91 m (298.5 ft); depth 6.8 m (22.3 ft)
Max. speed *(in standard atmosphere)*: 2,000 kph (1,240 mph)
Max. acceleration *(in space)*: 2,500G
Power: main reactor peak 3×10^{12} megawatts; peak shielding 6×10^{12} megawatts
Hyperdrive: Nubian 288 cores; S-6 generators (class 0.7; range 80,000 light years fully fuelled)
Crew: 1 pilot; 1 co-pilot; 3 others optional (navigator/comscan/shield operator); 5 astromech droids
Passengers: 4 prestige passengers; 6 guards
Armament: none

DARING ASSASSINATION

When a death-dealing explosion blows apart the Cruiser as it lands on Coruscant, Captain Typho assumes at first that a timed device must have been hidden onboard the ship. However, a more complete investigation points to a bomb on the landing platform itself having been remotely detonated. While Padmé suspects Separatist scare-tactics, Typho privately fears that high-placed insiders on Coruscant must have been involved for the tight security around the Naboo delegation to be breached so successfully.

Cables ground shield sinks to general power network

Deflector-shield generator and ray-shield emitter

Shield-receiver heat sinks and cooling radiators

Landing gear fairing

Main hold

Hyperdrive-navicomputer control links

Boarding ramp

Cargo cases

Power transmission for shield generator

Stern deflector shield projectors

Hyperdrive maintenance access hatch

Turbolift to crew deck

Maintenance Droids

Shield generator maintenance access hatch

RELIABLE TRANSPORT

As a leading emissary, Padmé has relied on her graceful diplomatic ship on scores of missions placating disgruntled factions throughout her sector. Even in this sturdy vessel, however, a thorough home constituency tour could last a lifetime in Padmé's lightly populated Chommell Sector, which comprises 36 full-member worlds, more than 40,000 settled dependencies, and 300,000,000 barren stars. With more than 1,000 sectors, the galaxy's deceptively fragile harmony depends on efficient divisions of authority within the multi-tiered government, and upon the wisdom of its roving officials and legislators.

Starfighter docked in recharge socket

IN-FLIGHT SUPPORT

Hyperdrive-capable starfighters are naturally limited by fuel capacity to jumps of less than 1,000 light-years. Previously, Naboo N-1 fighters operating far from home could only travel in small steps, accompanied by a tanker. After the invasion of Naboo, designers added innovative recharge sockets to the wings of the new diplomatic barge, thereby enabling the ship to carry its own security escort through hyperspace.

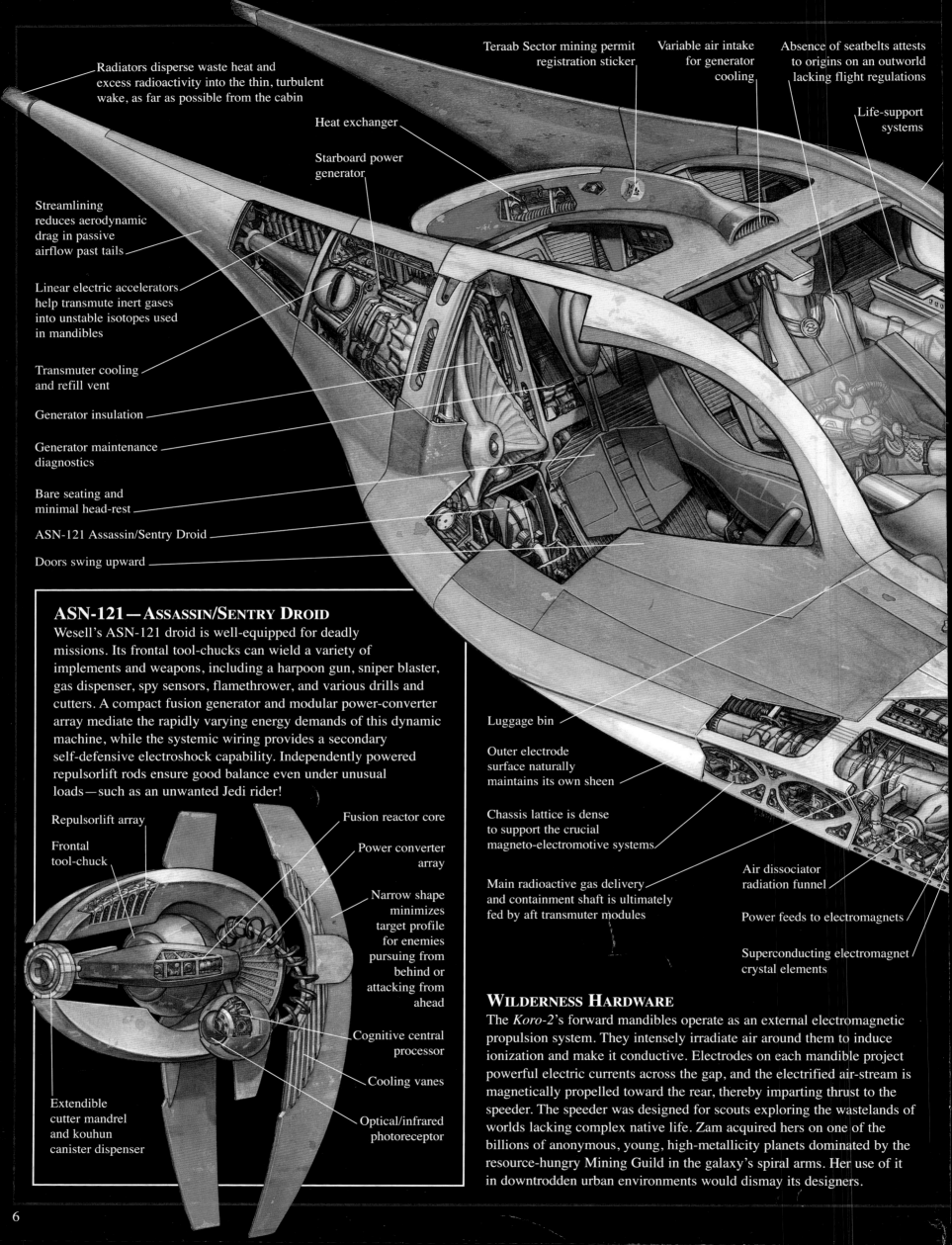

Radiators disperse waste heat and excess radioactivity into the thin, turbulent wake, as far as possible from the cabin

Heat exchanger

Starboard power generator

Teraab Sector mining permit registration sticker

Variable air intake for generator cooling

Absence of seatbelts attests to origins on an outworld lacking flight regulations

Life-support systems

Streamlining reduces aerodynamic drag in passive airflow past tails

Linear electric accelerators help transmute inert gases into unstable isotopes used in mandibles

Transmuter cooling and refill vent

Generator insulation

Generator maintenance diagnostics

Bare seating and minimal head-rest

ASN-121 Assassin/Sentry Droid

Doors swing upward

ASN-121—ASSASSIN/SENTRY DROID

Wesell's ASN-121 droid is well-equipped for deadly missions. Its frontal tool-chucks can wield a variety of implements and weapons, including a harpoon gun, sniper blaster, gas dispenser, spy sensors, flamethrower, and various drills and cutters. A compact fusion generator and modular power-converter array mediate the rapidly varying energy demands of this dynamic machine, while the systemic wiring provides a secondary self-defensive electroshock capability. Independently powered repulsorlift rods ensure good balance even under unusual loads—such as an unwanted Jedi rider!

Repulsorlift array

Frontal tool-chuck

Fusion reactor core

Power converter array

Narrow shape minimizes target profile for enemies pursuing from behind or attacking from ahead

Cognitive central processor

Cooling vanes

Extendible cutter mandrel and kouhun canister dispenser

Optical/infrared photoreceptor

Luggage bin

Outer electrode surface naturally maintains its own sheen

Chassis lattice is dense to support the crucial magneto-electromotive systems

Main radioactive gas delivery and containment shaft is ultimately fed by aft transmuter modules

Air dissociator radiation funnel

Power feeds to electromagnets

Superconducting electromagnet crystal elements

WILDERNESS HARDWARE

The *Koro-2*'s forward mandibles operate as an external electromagnetic propulsion system. They intensely irradiate air around them to induce ionization and make it conductive. Electrodes on each mandible project powerful electric currents across the gap, and the electrified air-stream is magnetically propelled toward the rear, thereby imparting thrust to the speeder. The speeder was designed for scouts exploring the wastelands of worlds lacking complex native life. Zam acquired hers on one of the billions of anonymous, young, high-metallicity planets dominated by the resource-hungry Mining Guild in the galaxy's spiral arms. Her use of it in downtrodden urban environments would dismay its designers.

ZAM'S AIRSPEEDER

HIRED ASSASSIN ZAM WESELL flies an airspeeder that is as unusual and exotic as she is herself. The totally self-enclosed craft has no external thrusters and few air intakes because it was built for use on hostile, primitive worlds. Its repulsorlift units provide anti-gravity support, while other mechanisms generate radiation and electromagnetic fields that move the craft by dragging upon the air. This system is versatile enough for use in a huge variety of atmospheres. However, in urban areas, outdoor power lines can snag the propulsion fields and confound the steering—although this merely provides an extra means of traction to a cunning mercenary like Wesell.

passes the cabin surface

Steering yokes control repulsorlift balance for banking turns

Dashboard navigation controls

Compartment holds special oils for shape-shifting Clawdites

Status lights indicate cabin non-contamination

Control displays

Pedals control power to mandible propulsion systems

Repulsorlift elements (under floor)

Fluorescent elements under translucent skin sense activity levels within operational ranges

Propulsion power systems, expanded upon standard model, protrude into mandible gap

Elongated storage bin for sniper rifle

Inner front surfaces have maximum piping density to provide the most intense irradiation

Maintenance log capsule

Inner electrode surface

Re-transmuter refreshes radioactivity during idle periods

Pump circulates radioactive fluid

Inner electrode anti-surge sink

Forward-scanner ranging device

Isolation shroud protects scanner

Propulsion system power cells

Vertical internal radiation shield

Irradiation gas distributor pipes

Shielded data cables connect frontal instruments to cabin controls

Forward power cells

Adaptive tuner regulates performance of right mandible propulsion systems

DATA FILE
Manufacturer: Desler Gizh Outworld Mobility Corp.
Make: *Koro-2* all-environment exodrive airspeeder
Dimensions: length 6.6 m (21.7 ft); width 2.1 m (7 ft); depth 0.9 m (3 ft)
Max. speed: 800 kph (496 mph)
Cargo capacity: 80 kg (176 lbs) or 0.04 m³ (1.4 ft³) in cabin and storage bins
Consumables: approx. five years' gas for irradiation system; two weeks' cabin air supply
Passengers: 1 (excluding driver)
Armament: none

DIRTY TECHNOLOGY

Zam's speeder creates some hazardous side-effects that amuse the callous hunter. Irradiation zones are constrained around the mandibles, but can sicken unknowing bystanders along the vehicle's path. Furthermore, drag-stream ions recombine chemically into unpleasant forms as they pass the cabin. In breathable atmospheres the products can include noxious gases that leave a foul reek in the speeder's wake.

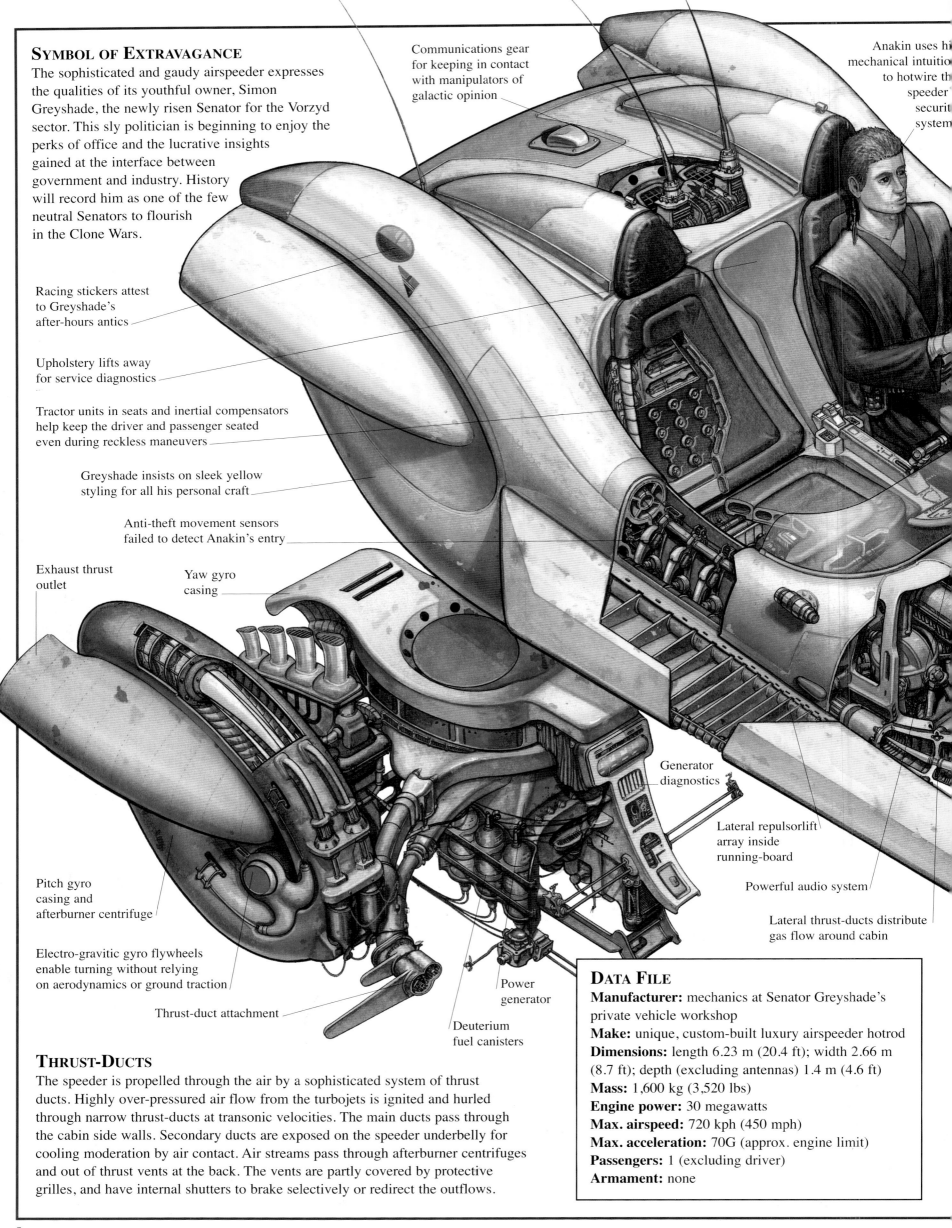

SYMBOL OF EXTRAVAGANCE

The sophisticated and gaudy airspeeder expresses the qualities of its youthful owner, Simon Greyshade, the newly risen Senator for the Vorzyd sector. This sly politician is beginning to enjoy the perks of office and the lucrative insights gained at the interface between government and industry. History will record him as one of the few neutral Senators to flourish in the Clone Wars.

Racing stickers attest to Greyshade's after-hours antics

Upholstery lifts away for service diagnostics

Tractor units in seats and inertial compensators help keep the driver and passenger seated even during reckless maneuvers

Greyshade insists on sleek yellow styling for all his personal craft

Anti-theft movement sensors failed to detect Anakin's entry

Communications gear for keeping in contact with manipulators of galactic opinion

Anakin uses hi mechanical intuitio to hotwire th speeder' securit system

Exhaust thrust outlet

Yaw gyro casing

Pitch gyro casing and afterburner centrifuge

Electro-gravitic gyro flywheels enable turning without relying on aerodynamics or ground traction

Thrust-duct attachment

Power generator

Deuterium fuel canisters

Generator diagnostics

Lateral repulsorlift array inside running-board

Powerful audio system

Lateral thrust-ducts distribute gas flow around cabin

THRUST-DUCTS

The speeder is propelled through the air by a sophisticated system of thrust ducts. Highly over-pressured air flow from the turbojets is ignited and hurled through narrow thrust-ducts at transonic velocities. The main ducts pass through the cabin side walls. Secondary ducts are exposed on the speeder underbelly for cooling moderation by air contact. Air streams pass through afterburner centrifuges and out of thrust vents at the back. The vents are partly covered by protective grilles, and have internal shutters to brake selectively or redirect the outflows.

DATA FILE

Manufacturer: mechanics at Senator Greyshade's private vehicle workshop
Make: unique, custom-built luxury airspeeder hotrod
Dimensions: length 6.23 m (20.4 ft); width 2.66 m (8.7 ft); depth (excluding antennas) 1.4 m (4.6 ft)
Mass: 1,600 kg (3,520 lbs)
Engine power: 30 megawatts
Max. airspeed: 720 kph (450 mph)
Max. acceleration: 70G (approx. engine limit)
Passengers: 1 (excluding driver)
Armament: none

ANAKIN'S AIRSPEEDER

AFTER AN ATTEMPT IS MADE ON THE LIFE of the Senator of Naboo and his Jedi Master is whisked off into the night air, Anakin Skywalker needs transport fast. With flawless intuition, he finds the perfect pursuit vehicle in the nearby Senatorial parking zone. This overpowered, prized leisure craft, which belongs to a self-indulgent politician, is as quick and agile as any civilian airspeeder or cloud car in Coruscant's sky. Its complex and responsive system of repulsor units, thrust-ducting, and unconventional Podracer-like engine arrangement provide one of the galaxy's best starpilots with the balance of superior control and instant familiarity essential for his daredevil pursuit of Zam Wesell.

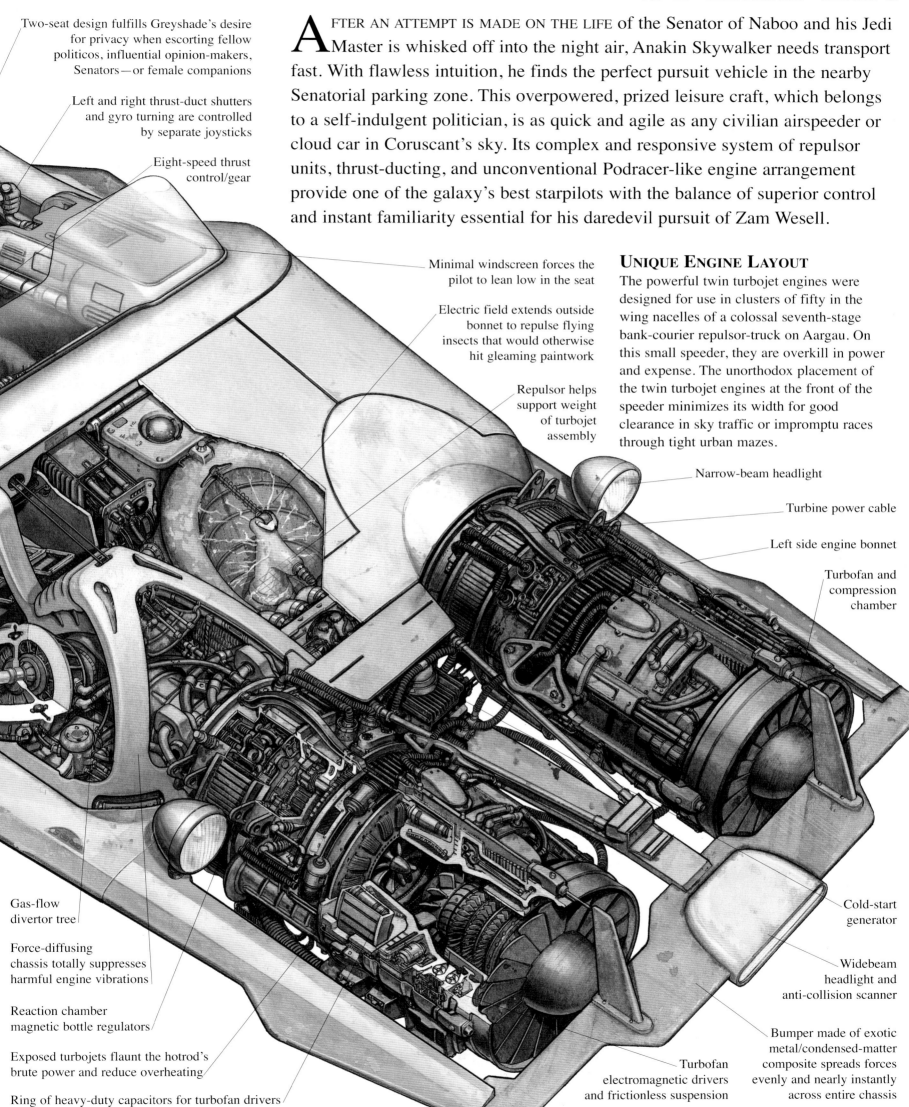

Two-seat design fulfills Greyshade's desire for privacy when escorting fellow politicos, influential opinion-makers, Senators—or female companions

Left and right thrust-duct shutters and gyro turning are controlled by separate joysticks

Eight-speed thrust control/gear

Minimal windscreen forces the pilot to lean low in the seat

Electric field extends outside bonnet to repulse flying insects that would otherwise hit gleaming paintwork

Repulsor helps support weight of turbojet assembly

UNIQUE ENGINE LAYOUT

The powerful twin turbojet engines were designed for use in clusters of fifty in the wing nacelles of a colossal seventh-stage bank-courier repulsor-truck on Aargau. On this small speeder, they are overkill in power and expense. The unorthodox placement of the twin turbojet engines at the front of the speeder minimizes its width for good clearance in sky traffic or impromptu races through tight urban mazes.

Narrow-beam headlight

Turbine power cable

Left side engine bonnet

Turbofan and compression chamber

Gas-flow divertor tree

Force-diffusing chassis totally suppresses harmful engine vibrations

Reaction chamber magnetic bottle regulators

Exposed turbojets flaunt the hotrod's brute power and reduce overheating

Ring of heavy-duty capacitors for turbofan drivers

Turbofan electromagnetic drivers and frictionless suspension

Cold-start generator

Widebeam headlight and anti-collision scanner

Bumper made of exotic metal/condensed-matter composite spreads forces evenly and nearly instantly across entire chassis

JEDI STARFIGHTER

When Obi-Wan Kenobi departs on his quest to Kamino, he requisitions one of the Jedi Temple's modified Delta-7 *Aethersprite* light interceptors. This ultra-light fighter is well shielded against impacts and blasts, and is equipped with two dual laser cannons that can unleash a withering frontal assault. Its sleek, blade-like form simplifies shield distribution and affords excellent visibility, especially in forward and lateral directions. A fighter of this size normally cannot travel far into deep space on its own, but the customized Jedi version features a socket for a truncated droid navigator and can dock with an external hyperdrive ring. Its design assumes dominance over any foe—essential for a prescient Jedi or any steely-nerved pilot trained for frontal assaults.

STOICAL DROID

Originally an R4-series astromech droid, R4-P17 was crushed while repairing trash compactor faults in the KDY research shipyards over Gyndine. While inspecting the Jedi customizations of the Delta-7 design, Anakin Skywalker found R4's wreck and rebuilt her with an R2-series dome. Now Temple property, R4 is the prototype for other integrated droid navigators in Jedi Delta-7 ships.

DATA FILE

Manufacturer: Kuat Systems Engineering, subsidiary of Kuat Drive Yards (fighter); TransGalMeg Industries Inc. (hyperdrive ring)
Make: Delta-7 *Aethersprite* light interceptor; Syliure-31 long-range hyperdrive module
Dimensions: length 8 m (26 ft); width 3.92 m (12.8 ft); depth 1.44 m (4.7 ft)
Max. speed *(in standard atmosphere)*: 12,000 kph (7,400 mph)
Max. acceleration *(linear, in open space)*: 5,000G
Hyperdrive: Class 1.0 (effective range 150,000 light-years)
Cargo capacity *(in cockpit)*: 60 kg (132 lbs) or 0.03 m³ (1.06 ft³)
Consumables: five hours' fuel and air in normal sublight operation (air supply prolonged if pilot uses Jedi hibernation trance)
Crew: 1 pilot and 1 modified, integrated astromech droid
Armament: 2 dual laser cannons (1 kiloton per shot max.)

ANCIENT ICON

The starboard wing of Obi-Wan's craft is marked with a symbol of a disc with eight spokes. This ancient icon dates to the Bendu monks' study of numerology wherein the number nine (eight spokes joined to one disc) signifies the beneficent presence of the Force in a unitary galaxy. After the fall of the Galactic Republic 1,000 generations later, the Emperor will personalize this symbol by defacing the icon with the removal of two spokes.

PRIVILEGED NETWORK SCOUT

In an emergency, Kenobi's ship can relay encrypted signals via any suitably powerful hyperwave transceiver located in the same planetary system. During the mission to Geonosis, Obi-Wan uses a powerful interstellar relay station in the Geonosis system to communicate with Anakin on Tatooine.

The fighter's tiny profile makes it difficult to detect and easy to hide from long-range sensors

Red coloration indicates Jedi plenipotentiary status and diplomatic immunity

Transformers and power cells for bow hardware

Firing groove

Power feeds to bow deflectors

Ancient roundel with eight spokes

Deflector shield power hub

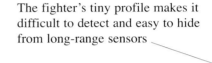

Comscan processor

Communications and scanning reflector dish

Multi-mode scanning and communications transceiver

Landing pad is a descending hull panel

Forward landing gear bay

Forward deflector shield projectors

Ventral landing claw enables docking in zero-gravity environments, such as on planetary ring boulders

Port landing light

Main reactor bulb

Laser cannon capacitors

Forward ventral power tree

Dual laser cannon emitter muzzles

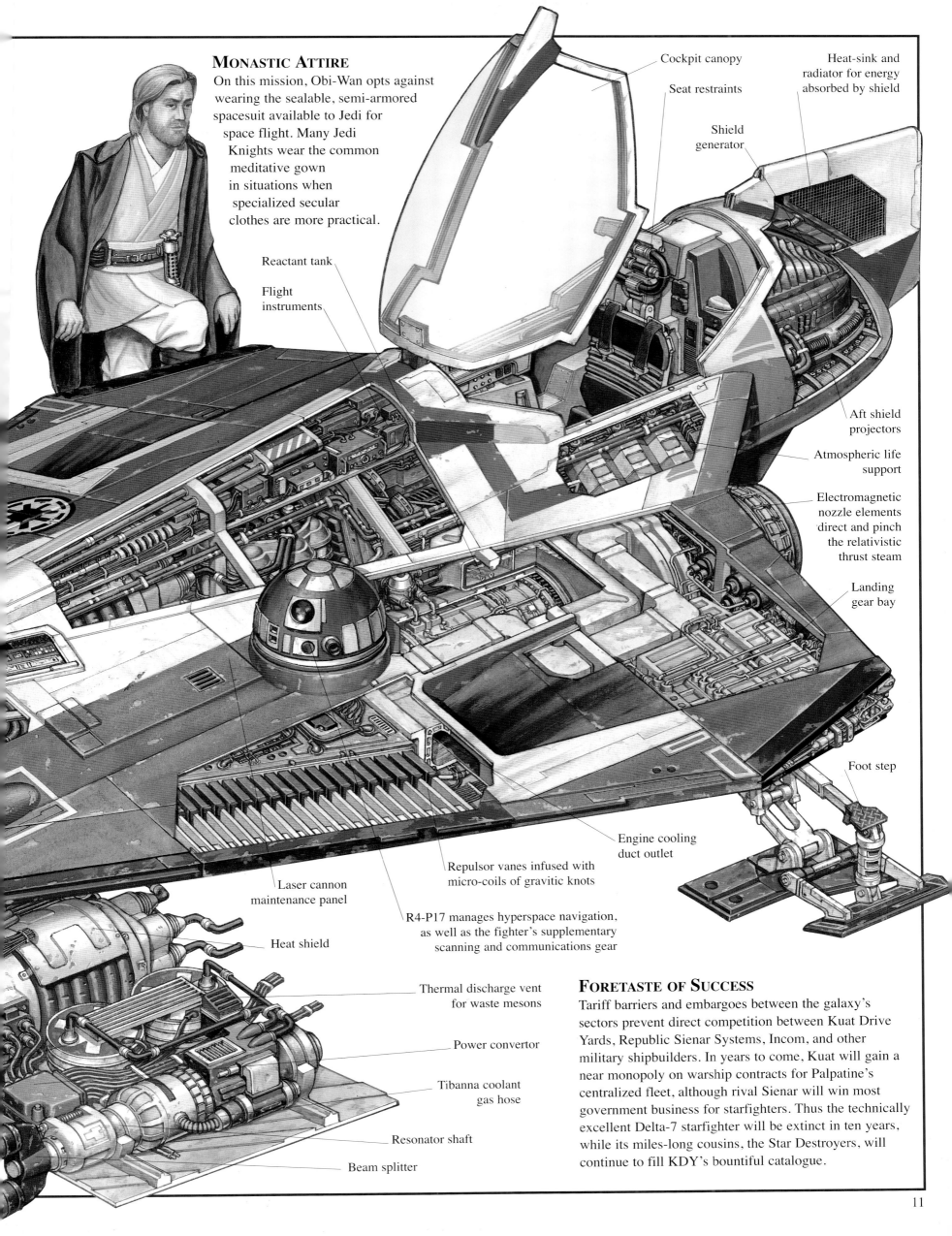

MONASTIC ATTIRE
On this mission, Obi-Wan opts against wearing the sealable, semi-armored spacesuit available to Jedi for space flight. Many Jedi Knights wear the common meditative gown in situations when specialized secular clothes are more practical.

Reactant tank

Flight instruments

Cockpit canopy

Seat restraints

Heat-sink and radiator for energy absorbed by shield

Shield generator

Aft shield projectors

Atmospheric life support

Electromagnetic nozzle elements direct and pinch the relativistic thrust steam

Landing gear bay

Foot step

Engine cooling duct outlet

Repulsor vanes infused with micro-coils of gravitic knots

Laser cannon maintenance panel

R4-P17 manages hyperspace navigation, as well as the fighter's supplementary scanning and communications gear

Heat shield

Thermal discharge vent for waste mesons

Power convertor

Tibanna coolant gas hose

Resonator shaft

Beam splitter

FORETASTE OF SUCCESS
Tariff barriers and embargoes between the galaxy's sectors prevent direct competition between Kuat Drive Yards, Republic Sienar Systems, Incom, and other military shipbuilders. In years to come, Kuat will gain a near monopoly on warship contracts for Palpatine's centralized fleet, although rival Sienar will win most government business for starfighters. Thus the technically excellent Delta-7 starfighter will be extinct in ten years, while its miles-long cousins, the Star Destroyers, will continue to fill KDY's bountiful catalogue.

SLAVE I

JANGO FETT PILOTS A VICIOUSLY EFFECTIVE, CUSTOMIZED STARSHIP with superior shielding combined with high endurance levels, and a heavy arsenal of overt and hidden weapons. At first glance, the rugged vessel is recognizable as an ordinary *Firespray*-class law-enforcement patrol ship. However, fine inspection reveals a montage of patched, rebuilt, and enhanced equipment attesting to its unsavory usage. Jango favors this uncommon but un-exotic craft for the element of disguise it affords him; as one of the galaxy's most proficient mercenaries, he nonetheless chooses to work in discreet obscurity, remaining unrecognized by most highly placed security officers and criminals alike.

When Jango's son Boba inherits *Slave I*, he will make some changes to suit his greater infamy and more aggressive style, including increased interstellar range and fuel capacity, installation of superior sensor jammers, and other stealth hardware.

DATA FILE

Manufacturer: Kuat Systems Engineering
Make: *Firespray*-class patrol and attack ship
Dimensions: length 21.5 m (70.5 ft); wingspan 21.3 m (70 ft); depth (excluding guns) 7.8 m (25.6 ft)
Max. speed (*in standard atmosphere*): 1,000 kph (620 mph)
Max. acceleration (*linear, in open space*): 2500G
Hyperdrive: class 1.0
Crew: 1 pilot; up to 2 co-pilots/navigator/gunners
Passengers: 2 seated (immobilized captives are stored in lockers)
Armament: 2 blaster cannons (600 gigajoules per shot); 2 laser cannons (8×10^{12} joules per shot); missile-launcher (8×10^{17} joules per shot); minelayer (5×10^{19} joules per shot); other unknown weapons

INTERIOR REFIT

Originally stolen by Jango on the asteroid prison Oovo IV, *Slave I* has been extensively modified after a few harsh space battles. Jango has added spartan crew quarters for long hunts, since the original *Firespray* was furnished for shorter-term patrols. In addition, the police-regulation prisoner cages have been converted into less-humane, coffin-like wall cabinets to ensure control of captives.

Fins contain repulsor grilles for landing maneuvers

Jango Fett

Cockpit console originally rotated to allow internal maintenance and observation of prisoner hold

Each deck's artificial gravity re-orients depending on flight mode

Flight instruments console

Boba Fett

Energy-shield shroud

Ladder to lower level

Corridor segment scavenged from a derelict Corellian starliner

Navigator station

Jango's bunk

Forward starboard reactant tank

Bunk sliding shutter

Atmospheric life-support

Forward shield generator destined for relocation to make room for larger power cells and fuel tanks

Shield generator main power conduit

Sublight communications antenna

Upper portside inertial compensator

Expansion grid for future hardware (Boba will install stealth gear)

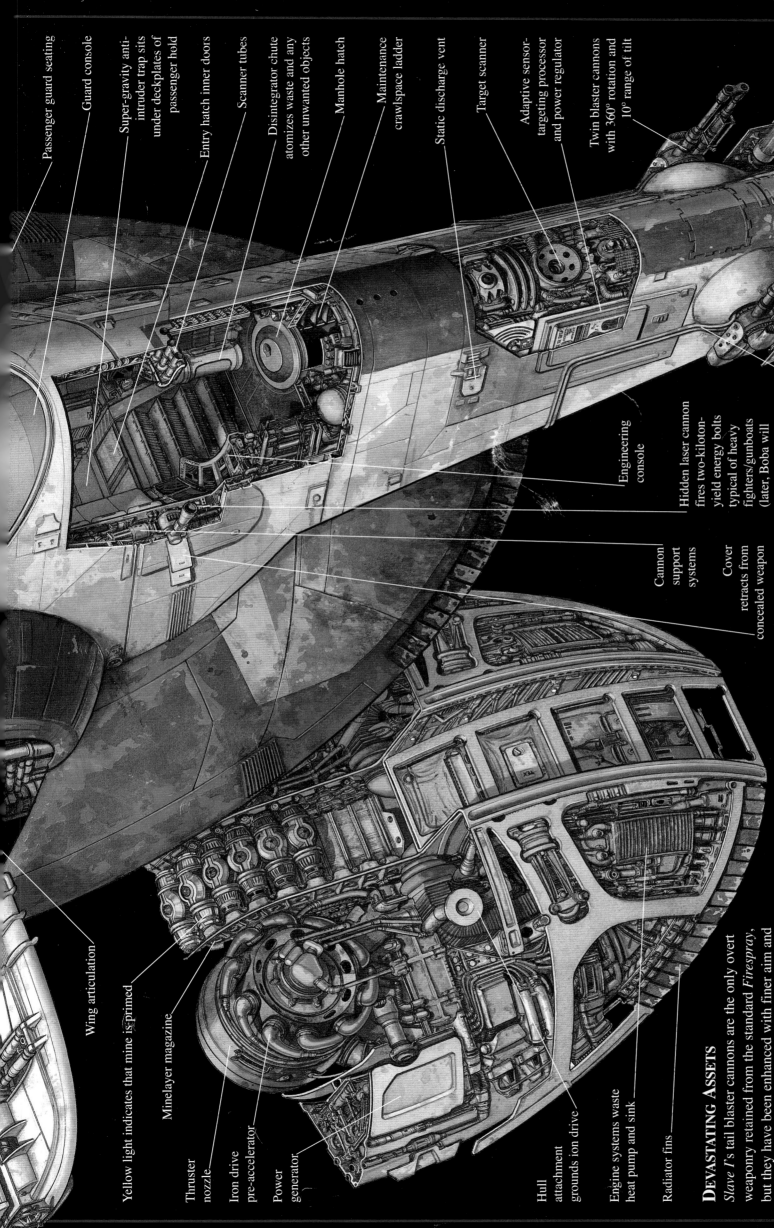

Passenger guard seating

Guard console

Super-gravity anti-intruder trap sits under deckplates of passenger hold

Entry hatch inner doors

Scanner tubes

Disintegrator chute atomizes waste and any other unwanted objects

Manhole hatch

Maintenance crawlspace ladder

Static discharge vent

Target scanner

Adaptive sensor-targeting processor and power regulator

Twin blaster cannons with 360° rotation and 10° range of tilt

Modified concussion missile inflicts blast-like kinetic effects without physical contact

Missile launcher under concealed panel

Missile launcher

Engineering console

Hidden laser cannon fires two-kiloton-yield energy bolts typical of heavy fighters/gunboats (later, Boba will replace it with an ion cannon for weapons diversity)

Makeshift external power lines feed tail cannons from a non-standard generator and capacitor array

Cannon support systems

Cover retracts from concealed weapon

Wing articulation

Yellow light indicates that mine is primed

Minelayer magazine

Thruster nozzle

Iron drive pre-accelerator

Power generator

Hull attachment grounds ion drive

Engine systems waste heat pump and sink

Radiator fins

DEVASTATING ASSETS

Slave I's tail blaster cannons are the only overt weaponry retained from the standard *Firespray*, but they have been enhanced with finer aim and variable power. Rapid-fire laser cannons concealed amidships have less control than the tail guns, but deliver kiloton-scale energy bolts at a greater rate. Fett has installed physical armaments as well: an adapted naval minelayer deals nasty surprises to hasty pursuers, and a concealed, frontal double-rack of torpedoes fulfils the role of a guided, heavy-assault weapon.

BAD FOR BUSINESS

The *Firespray* saw only limited production, as it was too heavily armed for civilian use yet was underpowered by Kuat's home-defense standards. Furthermore, *Firesprays* proved too robust, modular, and user-serviceable to support a profitable post-sale maintenance business. Although bad for the manufacturer, these characteristics make a perfect starship for an independent bounty hunter.

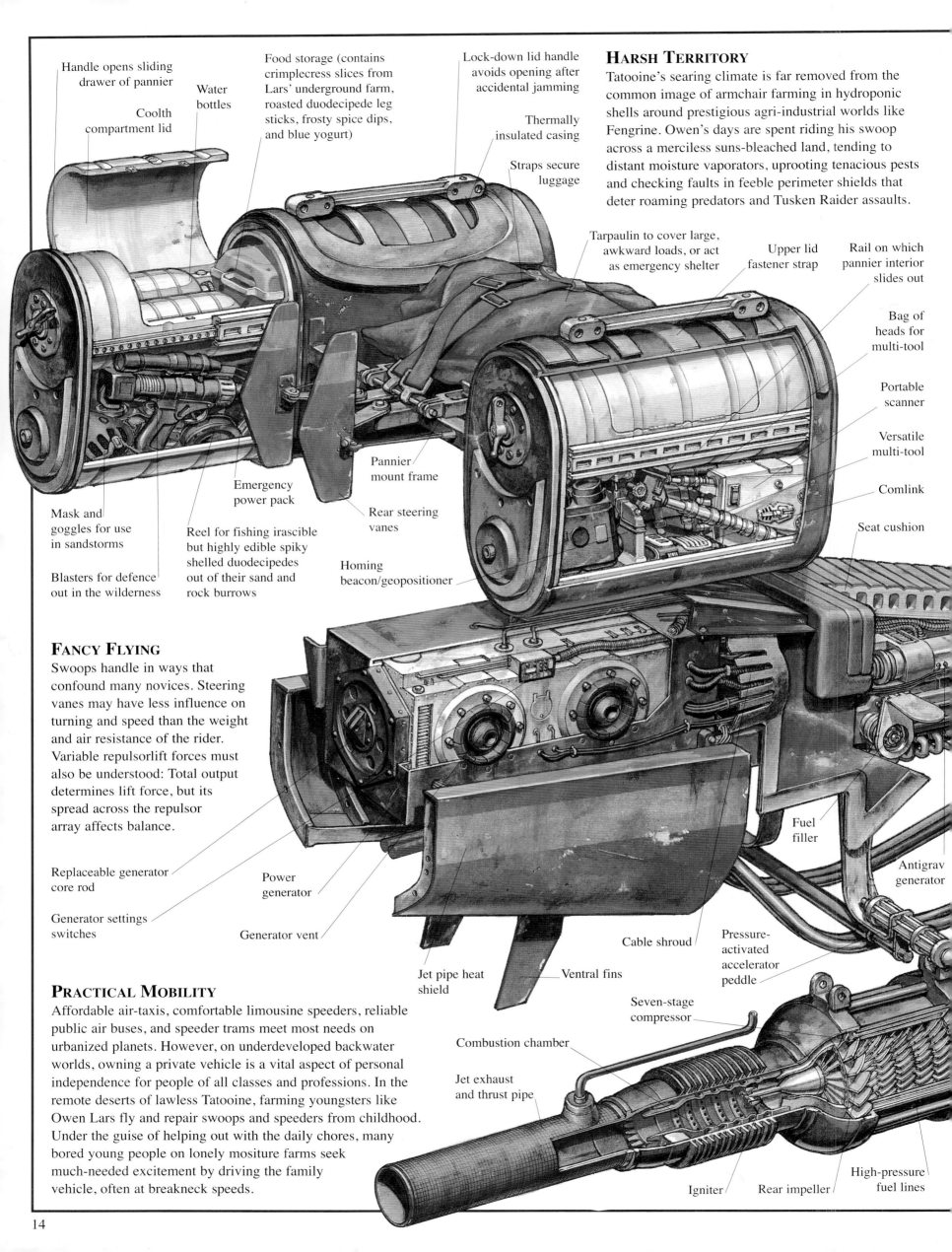

Handle opens sliding
drawer of pannier

Coolth
compartment lid

Water
bottles

Food storage (contains
crimplecress slices from
Lars' underground farm,
roasted duodecipede leg
sticks, frosty spice dips,
and blue yogurt)

Lock-down lid handle
avoids opening after
accidental jamming

Thermally
insulated casing

Straps secure
luggage

HARSH TERRITORY

Tatooine's searing climate is far removed from the
common image of armchair farming in hydroponic
shells around prestigious agri-industrial worlds like
Fengrine. Owen's days are spent riding his swoop
across a merciless suns-bleached land, tending to
distant moisture vaporators, uprooting tenacious pests
and checking faults in feeble perimeter shields that
deter roaming predators and Tusken Raider assaults.

Tarpaulin to cover large,
awkward loads, or act
as emergency shelter

Upper lid
fastener strap

Rail on which
pannier interior
slides out

Bag of
heads for
multi-tool

Portable
scanner

Versatile
multi-tool

Comlink

Seat cushion

Mask and
goggles for use
in sandstorms

Blasters for defence
out in the wilderness

Emergency
power pack

Reel for fishing irascible
but highly edible spiky
shelled duodecipedes
out of their sand and
rock burrows

Pannier
mount frame

Rear steering
vanes

Homing
beacon/geopositioner

FANCY FLYING

Swoops handle in ways that
confound many novices. Steering
vanes may have less influence on
turning and speed than the weight
and air resistance of the rider.
Variable repulsorlift forces must
also be understood: Total output
determines lift force, but its
spread across the repulsor
array affects balance.

Replaceable generator
core rod

Generator settings
switches

Power
generator

Generator vent

Fuel
filler

Antigrav
generator

Jet pipe heat
shield

Ventral fins

Cable shroud

Pressure-
activated
accelerator
peddle

PRACTICAL MOBILITY

Affordable air-taxis, comfortable limousine speeders, reliable
public air buses, and speeder trams meet most needs on
urbanized planets. However, on underdeveloped backwater
worlds, owning a private vehicle is a vital aspect of personal
independence for people of all classes and professions. In the
remote deserts of lawless Tatooine, farming youngsters like
Owen Lars fly and repair swoops and speeders from childhood.
Under the guise of helping out with the daily chores, many
bored young people on lonely moisture farms seek
much-needed excitement by driving the family
vehicle, often at breakneck speeds.

Seven-stage
compressor

Combustion chamber

Jet exhaust
and thrust pipe

Igniter

Rear impeller

High-pressure
fuel lines

OWEN LARS' SWOOP BIKE

Of all people on desolate Tatooine, the implacable moisture farmers have the most pragmatic appreciation of vehicular technology, upon which they depend for daily survival. Young Owen Lars epitomizes this principle, as he patrols the family property on his fast, sand-beaten swoop.

Though not especially reliable, this farm vehicle is used more heavily than the homestead's dozen other semi-restored craft because it is fuel-efficient and easy to repair using Jawa-supplied parts. Owen bought his high-powered swoop from a Revwien merchant at an auction in remote Mos Nytram. Originally a racing vehicle, he immediately saw its durable, practical use. Townsfolk might scoff at the sight of a onetime sports vehicle hauling water trailers or vermin traps, but as far as Owen is concerned, utility is the true essence of grace.

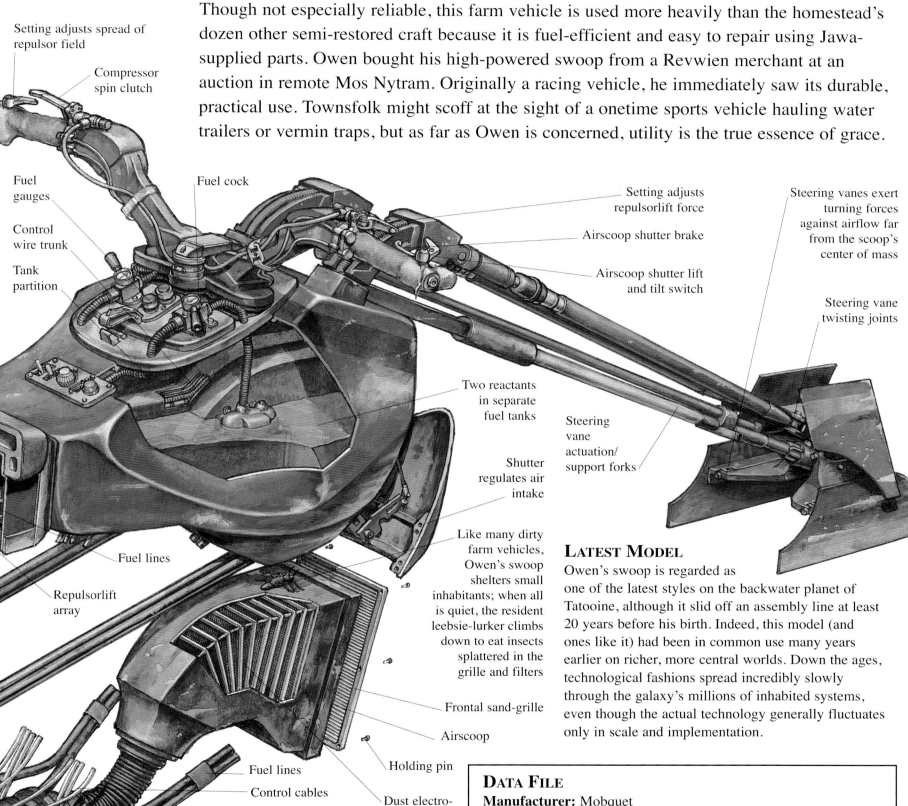

Setting adjusts spread of repulsor field

Compressor spin clutch

Fuel gauges

Control wire trunk

Fuel cock

Tank partition

Setting adjusts repulsorlift force

Airscoop shutter brake

Airscoop shutter lift and tilt switch

Steering vanes exert turning forces against airflow far from the scoop's center of mass

Steering vane twisting joints

Two reactants in separate fuel tanks

Steering vane actuation/ support forks

Shutter regulates air intake

Fuel lines

Repulsorlift array

Like many dirty farm vehicles, Owen's swoop shelters small inhabitants; when all is quiet, the resident leebsie-lurker climbs down to eat insects splattered in the grille and filters

Frontal sand-grille

Airscoop

Holding pin

Fuel lines

Control cables

Fuel mixing chamber

Front impeller

Dust electro-filter elements

LATEST MODEL

Owen's swoop is regarded as one of the latest styles on the backwater planet of Tatooine, although it slid off an assembly line at least 20 years before his birth. Indeed, this model (and ones like it) had been in common use many years earlier on richer, more central worlds. Down the ages, technological fashions spread incredibly slowly through the galaxy's millions of inhabited systems, even though the actual technology generally fluctuates only in scale and implementation.

SWOOP ENGINE

In its functional simplicity, the swoop is a tube. At the front, an airscoop feeds a turbojet in which fuel is mixed and ignited. At the rear, a tail-piped exhaust stream provides thrust. A repulsor array under the seat keeps the bike aloft, and is sustained by basic power cells and a generator. The only moving parts are the fans and gears of the compressor. These mechanisms are protected from abrasive sand and dust contaminants by a coarse grille at the airscoop mouth, followed by multiple layers of fast-acting electrostatic filters.

DATA FILE

Manufacturer: Mobquet
Make: Zephyr-G
Dimensions: length 3.68 m (12 ft); width 0.66 m (2 ft); depth 0.72 m (2.4 ft)
Max. airspeed: 350 kph (217 mph)
Max. acceleration: 2G (no inertial compensator; limited only by rider's grip and stamina!)
Cargo capacity: 50 kg (110 lbs) per pannier; 200 kg (440 lbs) lifting capacity including rider
Consumables: approx. 3,000 km (1,860 miles) worth of fuel
Crew: 1 (and 1 passenger, in discomfort)
Armament: none

PADMÉ'S STARSHIP

This slim yacht from the royal hangars of Naboo is not a spacious diplomatic platform for long-range tours and conferences. It is a relatively fast ship suited to discreet getaways. Its security features include a powerful Naboo-style shield system, electronic countermeasures, and a last-resort passenger escape capsule. Queen Jamillia's royal starships normally sit idle since she prefers to concentrate on Naboo's domestic affairs, entrusting her external powers to Senator Padmé Amidala. Thus, the smallest royal yacht is available and ideally suited for Padmé's undercover travels as the galaxy's most threatened political target. Its small crew requirements minimize the risk of sabotage, allowing Padmé and Anakin to pilot the ship alone with back-up flight assistance from the droids C-3PO and R2-D2. The yacht serves Padmé and Anakin well in their dangerous journey from Tatooine to the neighboring Geonosis system.

Coolant pump circulates a superfluid with enormous heat capacity to moderate the shield matrix during critical power spikes that cannot be radiated away quickly

Gleaming hull plating acts as passive physical radiation shielding

Deflector shield projector modules

Shield heat-sink and radiator matrix converts unusable energy surges into heat for disposal

Shield generator

Tube containing turbolift platform connects upper and lower deck for fast access

Navicomputer housing and power trunk

Navigator station

Anakin

Auxiliary comscan station

Anakin's crew bunk

Ship's manual

Toolkit

Main reactor

Galley

Orderly and aesthetically arranged Naboo circuitry

Astromech droid hold (two stations)

Connection to main reactor above

Starboard antigrav generator

Power node

Power trunk starboard fork

Extended boarding ramp

Starboard stern repulsor coils

Reactor fuel tank

Fuel baffles

R2-D2's station (unused)

Stores

Airlock

Hull substrate

INCONSPICUOUS TRANSPORT
The yacht is the smallest non-fighter vessel kept in the hangars of Theed Palace. Its simplified systems reduce maintenance time, making it ideal for secretive, unsupported excursions. It is much faster than most other civilian ships, and its narrow profile and sheltered engines amount to a small sensor signature. Thus the ship is well suited for evading the grasp of shadowy pursuers.

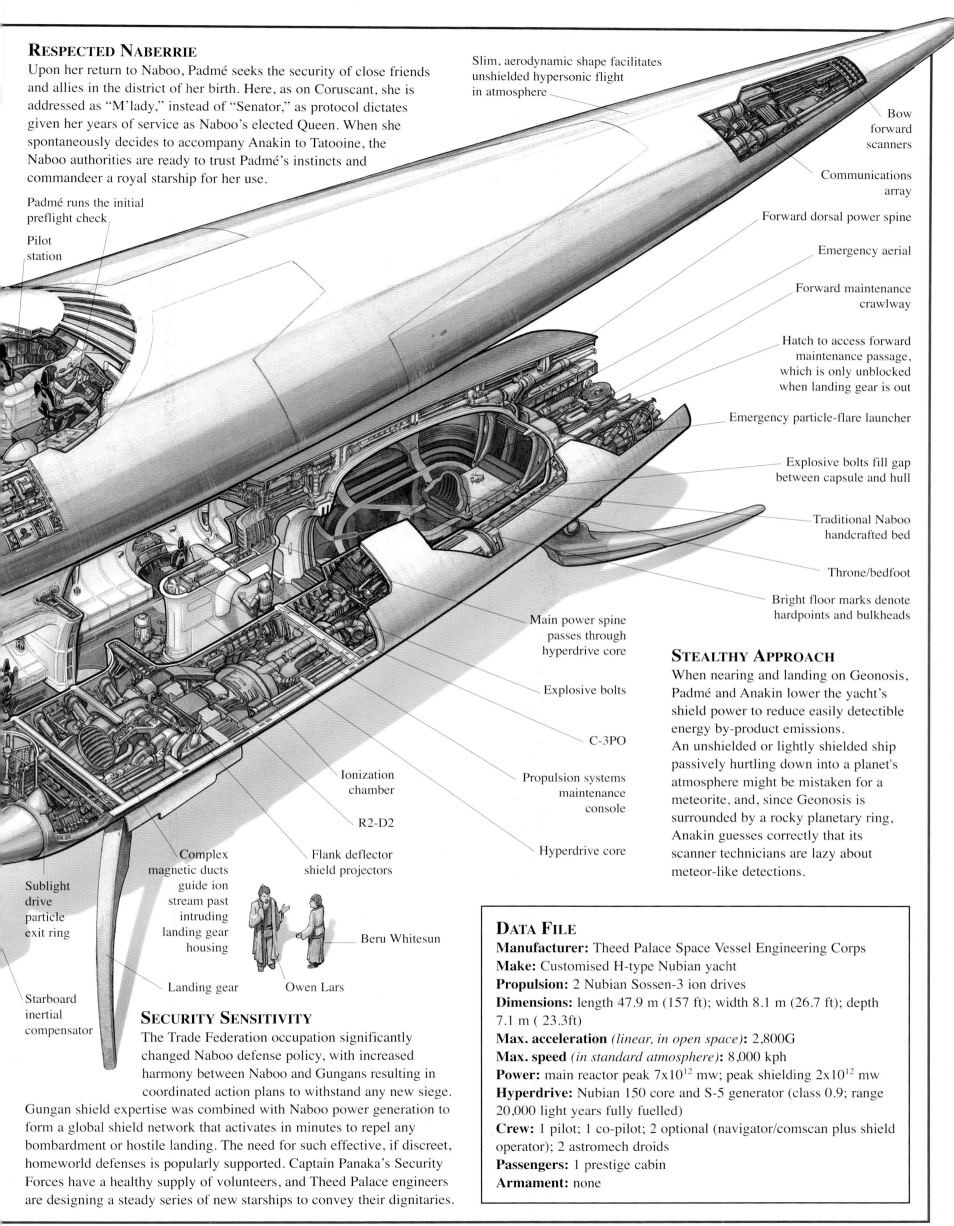

RESPECTED NABERRIE

Upon her return to Naboo, Padmé seeks the security of close friends and allies in the district of her birth. Here, as on Coruscant, she is addressed as "M'lady," instead of "Senator," as protocol dictates given her years of service as Naboo's elected Queen. When she spontaneously decides to accompany Anakin to Tatooine, the Naboo authorities are ready to trust Padmé's instincts and commandeer a royal starship for her use.

Padmé runs the initial preflight check

Pilot station

Sublight drive particle exit ring

Starboard inertial compensator

Complex magnetic ducts guide ion stream past intruding landing gear housing

Landing gear

Owen Lars

Beru Whitesun

Flank deflector shield projectors

R2-D2

Ionization chamber

Main power spine passes through hyperdrive core

Explosive bolts

C-3PO

Propulsion systems maintenance console

Hyperdrive core

Slim, aerodynamic shape facilitates unshielded hypersonic flight in atmosphere

Bow forward scanners

Communications array

Forward dorsal power spine

Emergency aerial

Forward maintenance crawlway

Hatch to access forward maintenance passage, which is only unblocked when landing gear is out

Emergency particle-flare launcher

Explosive bolts fill gap between capsule and hull

Traditional Naboo handcrafted bed

Throne/bedfoot

Bright floor marks denote hardpoints and bulkheads

STEALTHY APPROACH

When nearing and landing on Geonosis, Padmé and Anakin lower the yacht's shield power to reduce easily detectible energy by-product emissions. An unshielded or lightly shielded ship passively hurtling down into a planet's atmosphere might be mistaken for a meteorite, and, since Geonosis is surrounded by a rocky planetary ring, Anakin guesses correctly that its scanner technicians are lazy about meteor-like detections.

SECURITY SENSITIVITY

The Trade Federation occupation significantly changed Naboo defense policy, with increased harmony between Naboo and Gungans resulting in coordinated action plans to withstand any new siege. Gungan shield expertise was combined with Naboo power generation to form a global shield network that activates in minutes to repel any bombardment or hostile landing. The need for such effective, if discreet, homeworld defenses is popularly supported. Captain Panaka's Security Forces have a healthy supply of volunteers, and Theed Palace engineers are designing a steady series of new starships to convey their dignitaries.

DATA FILE
Manufacturer: Theed Palace Space Vessel Engineering Corps
Make: Customised H-type Nubian yacht
Propulsion: 2 Nubian Sossen-3 ion drives
Dimensions: length 47.9 m (157 ft); width 8.1 m (26.7 ft); depth 7.1 m (23.3ft)
Max. acceleration (*linear, in open space*)**:** 2,800G
Max. speed (*in standard atmosphere*)**:** 8,000 kph
Power: main reactor peak $7x10^{12}$ mw; peak shielding $2x10^{12}$ mw
Hyperdrive: Nubian 150 core and S-5 generator (class 0.9; range 20,000 light years fully fuelled)
Crew: 1 pilot; 1 co-pilot; 2 optional (navigator/comscan plus shield operator); 2 astromech droids
Passengers: 1 prestige cabin
Armament: none

TRADE FEDERATION CORE SHIP

WITH ITS FLEETS OF FREIGHTER-BATTLESHIPS, the Trade Federation is well-equipped to be one of the powerful merchant factions behind the advent of the Clone Wars. The heart and brain of each battleship is a detachable Core Ship, which comprizes a massive, central computer and multiple power systems. These huge ships are serviced in special landing pits on planets minus transmission mast) 914 m (3,000 ft). The Core Ships' ion-drive nozzles provide basic steering and slow acceleration, allowing them to dock in powerful, anti-gravity repulsorlift cushions with eight landing legs for stability. Scores of these ships are grounded on Geonosis, where they are being upgraded for coordination with the newly enhanced Baktoid droid armies. During the battle on Geonosis, the Core Ships are ringed with land and air defenses, allowing a good number to retreat safely to the skies.

DATA FILE

Manufacturer: Hoersch-Kessel Drive Inc. (basic Core Ship); Baktoid Combat Automata (droid-army control core)

Model: *Lucrehulk*-class modular control core (LH-1740)

Dimensions: diameter 696 m (2285 ft); depth (when landed, minus transmission mast) 914 m (3,000 ft).

Max. acceleration *(linear, in open space)*: 300G

Power: reactor peak 3×10^{24} watts; peak shield capacity 6×10^{23} watts

Cargo capacity: approx. 66 million m³ (2.3 billion ft³)

Consumables: 3 years supplies

Crew: 60 Trade Federation supervisors; 3,000 Droid Crew; 200,000 Maintenance Droids

Passengers: stateroom capacity for 60,000 trade representatives

Armament: 280 point-defense light laser cannons (8 kilotons per shot max.)

VERTICAL ORGANIZATION

The hierachical arrangement of habitable areas on the Core Ships matches that of Neimoidian hives. Control bridges, executive suites, and treasuries are concentrated in globe's upper pole and towers, and resemble Neimoidia's luxurious surface palaces. Deeper levels are for junior managers, publicists, brokers, and droid storage. The lowest decks contain engineering areas and conference rooms for meeting outsiders; like the unfavorably dry and hot basements of Neimoidian warrens, frequented by subterranean scavengers and parasites, these decks are shunned by high-ranking officials.

Military Droid-feedback rectenna

Locking ridges on hull fit sockets on different classes of Trade Federation freighters and warships

Compact hypermatter-annihilation reactor

Newly upgraded AAT tanks loaded into equatorial bay

Transmitter tuning cells

Radiator cools transmission generators

Power generator supports transmitter sub-systems

Military control towers (now installed on most Core Ships)

Transmission mast for military feedback and control signals

Scanner array

Executive escape-pod bay

Command bridge

VIP treasury

Luxury executive suites

Upgraded computer core allows coordination of droid armies via Officer Droids and neighboring droid-control ships

Docking ring for Corellian-standard boarding tubes and airlocks

New secondary fuel silos improve reactor overload containment systems

STANDARD PART

Core-Ship design has changed little in the last century. In a typical display of Neimoidian thrift, the spheres can serve a variety of craft: The split-ring freighter-battleships of the Naboo blockade; larger, unarmed container vessels and tankers; and newer warships of the post-Naboo period, including cruisers with improved weapons placement and smaller, faster destroyers that defend the fleets and chase down blockade runners.

Ancilliary reactors

Reactor-support assemblies are independent fusion-powered triggers and confinement-field generators for the hypermatter main-reactor core

Trench shield projectors channel their energies in synchronous sheaths

Thermal exhaust-vent safely moderates heat surges in core

Shield generator

Ceremonial hall for signing treaties and planetary protectorship leases

Lower decks are mostly uninhabited but patrolled by security droids

C-9979 landing ship parts

MTT troop transports

Defensive artillery

Droid battalions

Boarding ramp

New storage holds added after full militarization

Retractable maintenance gantry

Power feeds recharge ship systems

Landing gear retractors

Faster-than-light "hyperwave" transceiver reaches any part of the galaxy directly without using public HoloNet relays

Hull sections from leg socket cover

Heavy cargo lift

Waste fluid vent

Artillery power generator

Observation stations and workshops

Lift shaft

Walls are lined with gravitational reflectors for the ship's repulsors to act against

Particle shields cycle and intensify in trenches

Small, point-defense turrets

Thruster blast and radiation are harmlessly channeled into 6.4-km (4-mile) deep shaft

Anti-gravity repulsorlift suspensors

Foot-pads have never been tested to support the ship's full weight without repulsorlift assistance for more than an hour

Ventral thruster extends out of a lower hatch

Rings project one-way force-field that contains harmful radiation from the ship's exhaust in the blast shaft

HYPERLANE CONTROL

Core Ships' navicomputers contain precious interstellar data charts. In bygone ages, governments and private agencies shared such information publicly, but now the Trade Federation aggressively protects the coordinates it owns. As changes in astronomical conditions can make routes unsafe, the Trade Federation is gaining a virtual transport monopoly over patches of the galaxy. Now, only the Jedi and the Office of the Supreme Chancellor can afford to maintain more comprehensive charts.

NEW ALLY

After more than a decade of promoting its own trade interests by underhand means, the Trade Federation recognizes the strategic value of Count Dooku. As a persuasive orator with a zealous following on thousands of Separatist worlds, including Geonosis (home to the Trade Federation's favorite dockyards and armorers), he is serving to increase disunity through the galaxy—and, as Nute Gunray knows, weak governments are good for business.

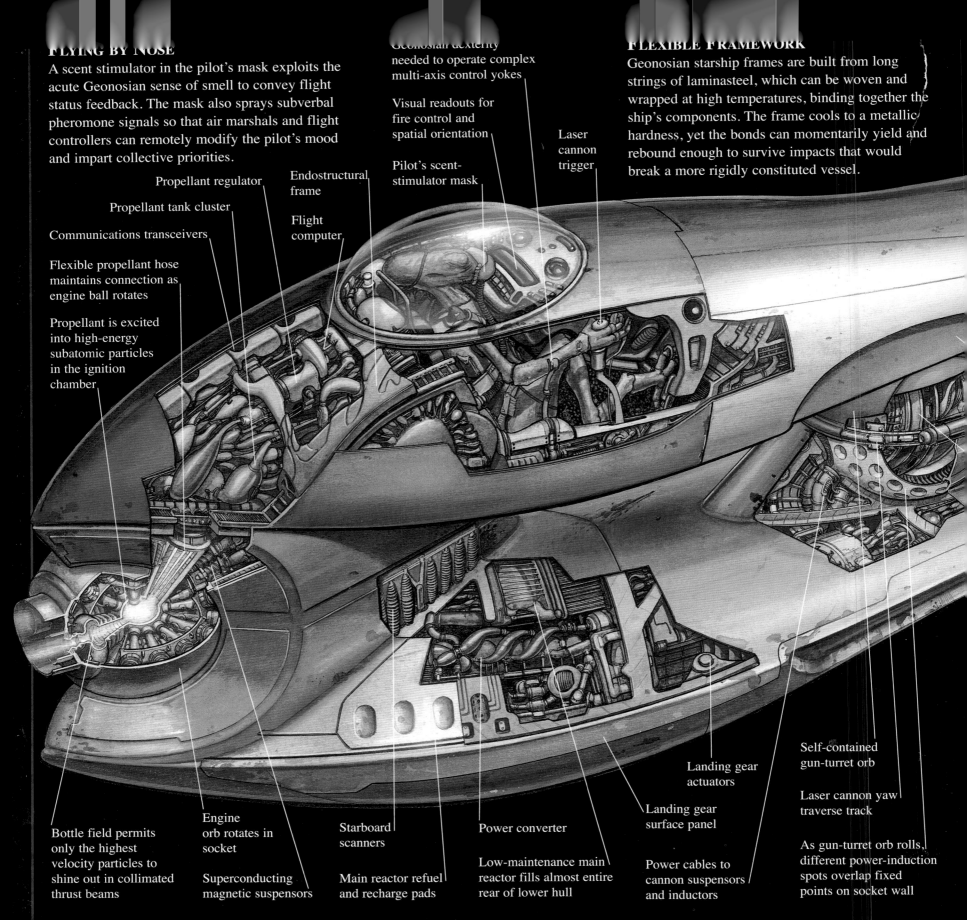

FLYING BY NOSE

A scent stimulator in the pilot's mask exploits the acute Geonosian sense of smell to convey flight status feedback. The mask also sprays subverbal pheromone signals so that air marshals and flight controllers can remotely modify the pilot's mood and impart collective priorities.

Geonosian dexterity needed to operate complex multi-axis control yokes

Visual readouts for fire control and spatial orientation

Pilot's scent-stimulator mask

Laser cannon trigger

FLEXIBLE FRAMEWORK

Geonosian starship frames are built from long strings of laminasteel, which can be woven and wrapped at high temperatures, binding together the ship's components. The frame cools to a metallic hardness, yet the bonds can momentarily yield and rebound enough to survive impacts that would break a more rigidly constituted vessel.

Propellant regulator

Propellant tank cluster

Communications transceivers

Endostructural frame

Flight computer

Flexible propellant hose maintains connection as engine ball rotates

Propellant is excited into high-energy subatomic particles in the ignition chamber

Self-contained gun-turret orb

Laser cannon yaw traverse track

Landing gear actuators

Landing gear surface panel

As gun-turret orb rolls, different power-induction spots overlap fixed points on socket wall

Power converter

Low-maintenance main reactor fills almost entire rear of lower hull

Power cables to cannon suspensors and inductors

Bottle field permits only the highest velocity particles to shine out in collimated thrust beams

Engine orb rotates in socket

Superconducting magnetic suspensors

Starboard scanners

Main reactor refuel and recharge pads

GEONOSIAN FIGHTER

DURING THE CLIMACTIC BATTLE WITH THE REPUBLIC, the Geonosian faction launches thousands of standby fighters to break the Republic's orbital cordon blocking Corporate Alliance ground reinforcements. These fightercraft combine high linear acceleration with phenomenal maneuverability as a result of the frictionless rotating mount of their thrusters. Despite their superior agility, few fighters are exported, since Geonosian senses and articulation differ from the galaxy's majority humanoid population. Furthermore, Geonosian policy has become fervently isolationist as the Republic stagnates, and their wary Archduke, Poggle the Lesser, believes that the hoarding of technical advantages is insurance of power and security.

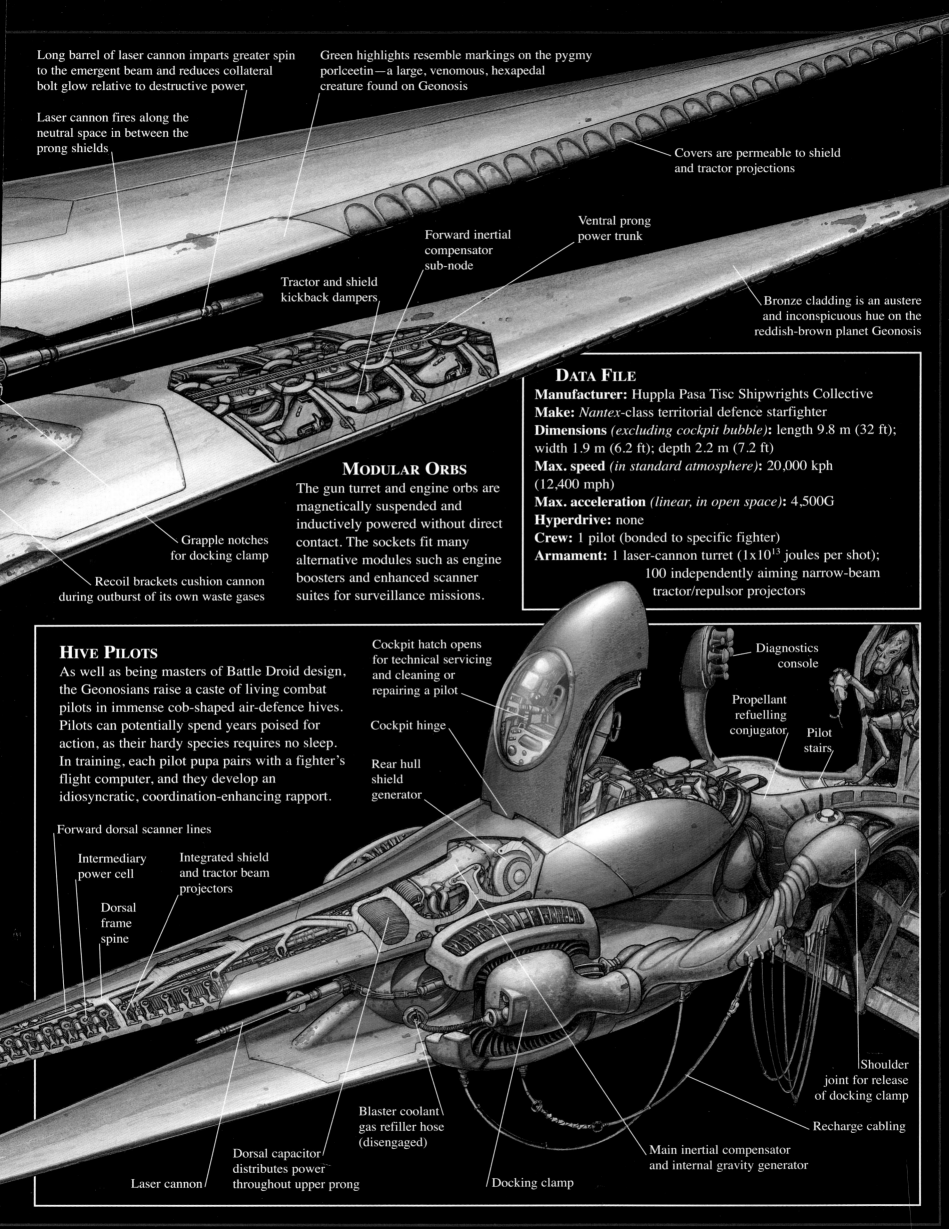

Long barrel of laser cannon imparts greater spin to the emergent beam and reduces collateral bolt glow relative to destructive power

Green highlights resemble markings on the pygmy porlceetin—a large, venomous, hexapedal creature found on Geonosis

Laser cannon fires along the neutral space in between the prong shields

Covers are permeable to shield and tractor projections

Ventral prong power trunk

Forward inertial compensator sub-node

Tractor and shield kickback dampers

Bronze cladding is an austere and inconspicuous hue on the reddish-brown planet Geonosis

MODULAR ORBS

The gun turret and engine orbs are magnetically suspended and inductively powered without direct contact. The sockets fit many alternative modules such as engine boosters and enhanced scanner suites for surveillance missions.

Grapple notches for docking clamp

Recoil brackets cushion cannon during outburst of its own waste gases

DATA FILE

Manufacturer: Huppla Pasa Tisc Shipwrights Collective
Make: *Nantex*-class territorial defence starfighter
Dimensions *(excluding cockpit bubble)*: length 9.8 m (32 ft); width 1.9 m (6.2 ft); depth 2.2 m (7.2 ft)
Max. speed *(in standard atmosphere)*: 20,000 kph (12,400 mph)
Max. acceleration *(linear, in open space)*: 4,500G
Hyperdrive: none
Crew: 1 pilot (bonded to specific fighter)
Armament: 1 laser-cannon turret (1×10^{13} joules per shot); 100 independently aiming narrow-beam tractor/repulsor projectors

HIVE PILOTS

As well as being masters of Battle Droid design, the Geonosians raise a caste of living combat pilots in immense cob-shaped air-defence hives. Pilots can potentially spend years poised for action, as their hardy species requires no sleep. In training, each pilot pupa pairs with a fighter's flight computer, and they develop an idiosyncratic, coordination-enhancing rapport.

Cockpit hatch opens for technical servicing and cleaning or repairing a pilot

Diagnostics console

Cockpit hinge

Propellant refuelling conjugator

Pilot stairs

Rear hull shield generator

Forward dorsal scanner lines

Intermediary power cell

Integrated shield and tractor beam projectors

Dorsal frame spine

Shoulder joint for release of docking clamp

Recharge cabling

Blaster coolant gas refiller hose (disengaged)

Dorsal capacitor distributes power throughout upper prong

Main inertial compensator and internal gravity generator

Laser cannon

Docking clamp

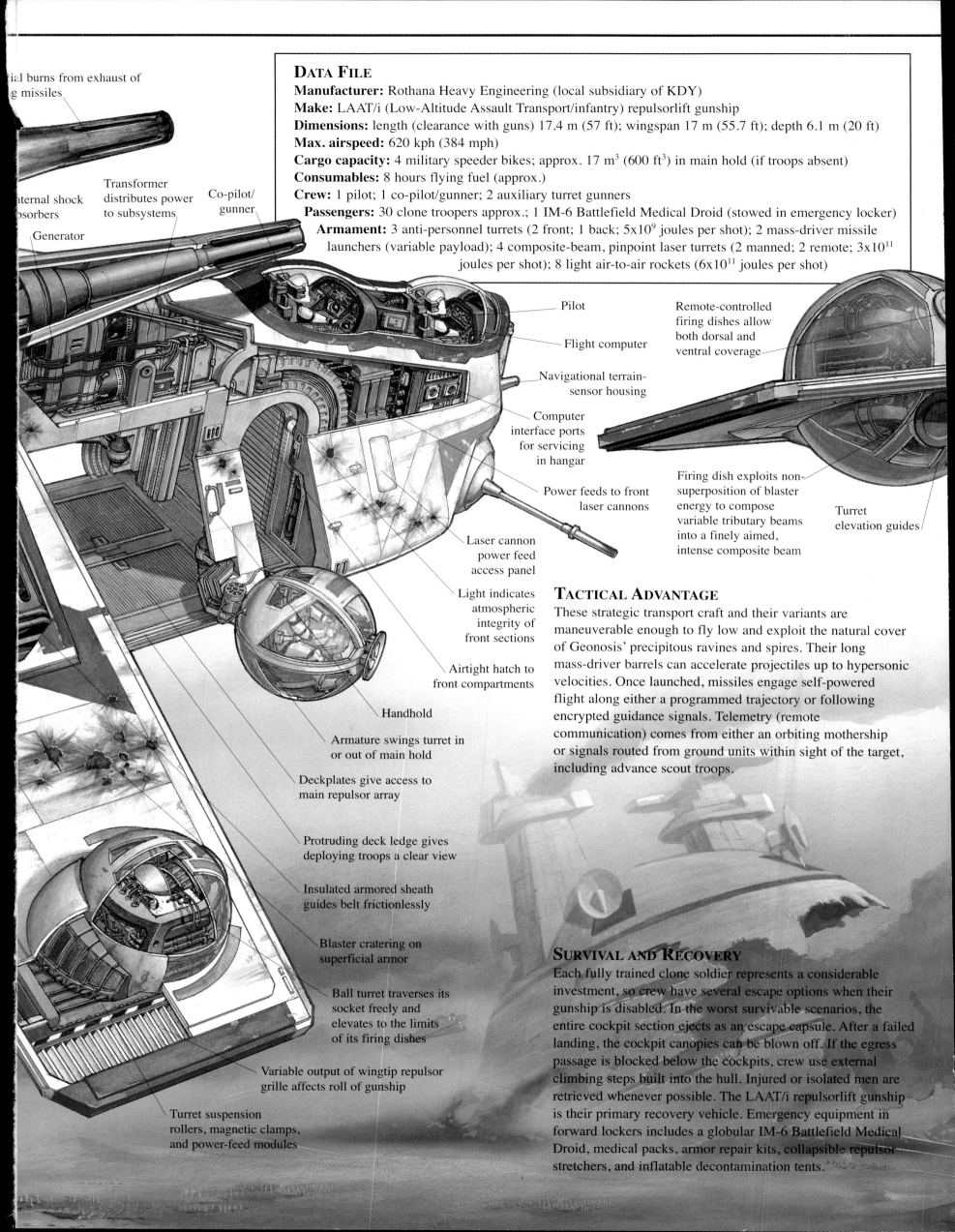

...ial burns from exhaust of ...g missiles

...ternal shock ...sorbers

Generator

Transformer distributes power to subsystems

Co-pilot/gunner

DATA FILE

Manufacturer: Rothana Heavy Engineering (local subsidiary of KDY)
Make: LAAT/i (Low-Altitude Assault Transport/infantry) repulsorlift gunship
Dimensions: length (clearance with guns) 17.4 m (57 ft); wingspan 17 m (55.7 ft); depth 6.1 m (20 ft)
Max. airspeed: 620 kph (384 mph)
Cargo capacity: 4 military speeder bikes; approx. 17 m³ (600 ft³) in main hold (if troops absent)
Consumables: 8 hours flying fuel (approx.)
Crew: 1 pilot; 1 co-pilot/gunner; 2 auxiliary turret gunners
Passengers: 30 clone troopers approx.; 1 IM-6 Battlefield Medical Droid (stowed in emergency locker)
Armament: 3 anti-personnel turrets (2 front; 1 back; 5×10^9 joules per shot); 2 mass-driver missile launchers (variable payload); 4 composite-beam, pinpoint laser turrets (2 manned; 2 remote; 3×10^{11} joules per shot); 8 light air-to-air rockets (6×10^{11} joules per shot)

Pilot

Flight computer

Navigational terrain-sensor housing

Computer interface ports for servicing in hangar

Power feeds to front laser cannons

Laser cannon power feed access panel

Light indicates atmospheric integrity of front sections

Airtight hatch to front compartments

Handhold

Armature swings turret in or out of main hold

Deckplates give access to main repulsor array

Protruding deck ledge gives deploying troops a clear view

Insulated armored sheath guides belt frictionlessly

Blaster cratering on superficial armor

Ball turret traverses its socket freely and elevates to the limits of its firing dishes

Variable output of wingtip repulsor grille affects roll of gunship

Turret suspension rollers, magnetic clamps, and power-feed modules

Remote-controlled firing dishes allow both dorsal and ventral coverage

Firing dish exploits non-superposition of blaster energy to compose variable tributary beams into a finely aimed, intense composite beam

Turret elevation guides

TACTICAL ADVANTAGE

These strategic transport craft and their variants are maneuverable enough to fly low and exploit the natural cover of Geonosis' precipitous ravines and spires. Their long mass-driver barrels can accelerate projectiles up to hypersonic velocities. Once launched, missiles engage self-powered flight along either a programmed trajectory or following encrypted guidance signals. Telemetry (remote communication) comes from either an orbiting mothership or signals routed from ground units within sight of the target, including advance scout troops.

SURVIVAL AND RECOVERY

Each fully trained clone soldier represents a considerable investment, so crew have several escape options when their gunship is disabled. In the worst survivable scenarios, the entire cockpit section ejects as an escape capsule. After a failed landing, the cockpit canopies can be blown off. If the egress passage is blocked below the cockpits, crew use external climbing steps built into the hull. Injured or isolated men are retrieved whenever possible. The LAAT/i repulsorlift gunship is their primary recovery vehicle. Emergency equipment in forward lockers includes a globular IM-6 Battlefield Medical Droid, medical packs, armor repair kits, collapsible repulsor stretchers, and inflatable decontamination tents.

DIVERSE ORDNANCE

The LAAT gunship's use of missiles and energy weapons provides complementary benefits. Whereas a blaster can almost instantly hit anything within a clear line of sight, a missile may go around obstacles and over the horizon. A missile can sometimes be dodged or shot down, while an energy beam cannot be intercepted, except by shield absorption. Missile payloads are variable and mission-specific. Different classes of missile optimize the fusion or annihilation explosion for specific effects, including a simple omnidirectional blast, a fan or beamed blast, a dispersal of a corrosive antimatter shower, electromagnetic pulse effects, a sterilizing burst of hard radiation, or concentrated heat effects.

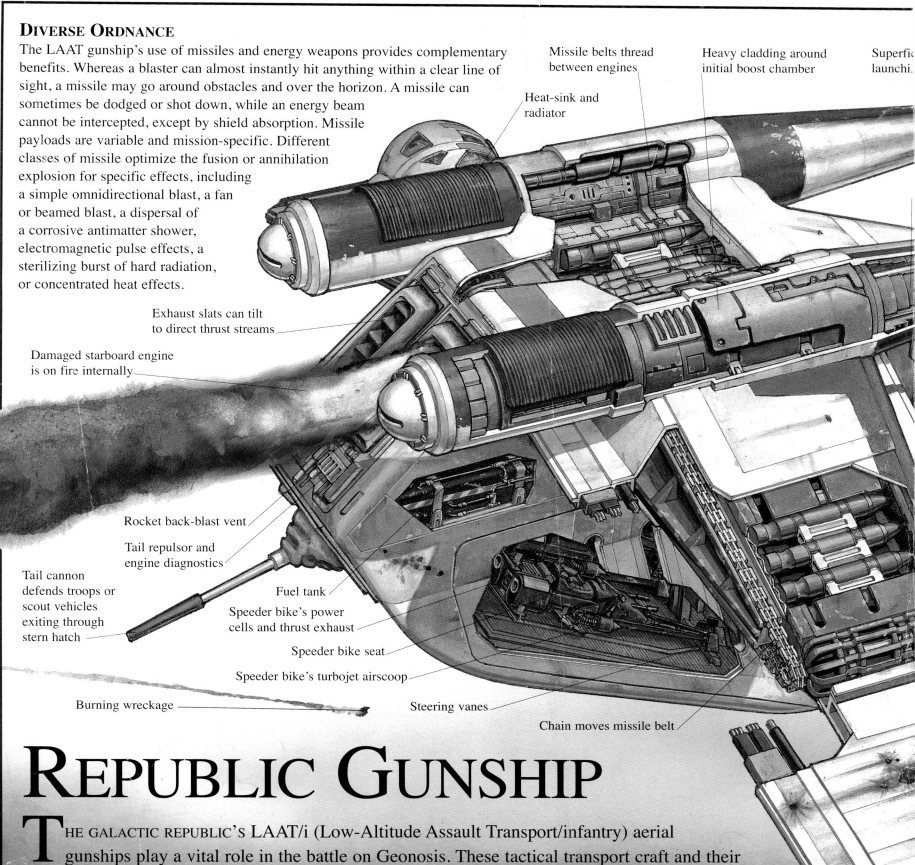

Missile belts thread between engines

Heavy cladding around initial boost chamber

Superfi launchi

Heat-sink and radiator

Exhaust slats can tilt to direct thrust streams

Damaged starboard engine is on fire internally

Rocket back-blast vent

Tail repulsor and engine diagnostics

Tail cannon defends troops or scout vehicles exiting through stern hatch

Fuel tank

Speeder bike's power cells and thrust exhaust

Speeder bike seat

Speeder bike's turbojet airscoop

Burning wreckage

Steering vanes

Chain moves missile belt

Power feeds to wing repulsors and turret

REPUBLIC GUNSHIP

THE GALACTIC REPUBLIC'S LAAT/i (Low-Altitude Assault Transport/infantry) aerial gunships play a vital role in the battle on Geonosis. These tactical transport craft and their variants can cross impassibly rough terrain to swiftly and safely disgorge an entire platoon of clone troopers or haul a slower armored vehicle into position. Enemy fighters must either remain at high altitudes or surrender their speed advantage when pursuing gunships below the mountain level. A military transport ship's entire gunship complement can deliver more than 2,000 soldiers in each of several repeated waves. However, these flying troop carriers are versatile gun platforms in their own right, too. They are lighter and faster than mobile artillery and most ground vehicles, yet still carry a considerable arsenal. Massive twin missile launchers allow concerted over-the-horizon strikes on slow or fixed targets such as enemy artillery and fortifications, in support of the advancing ground forces. Two pairs of widely rotating blaster cannons defend the gunship with bolts of deadly precision. Finally, three chin- and tail-mounted laser cannons swivel and depress to devastate enemy infantry and other light ground assets. These guns are vital for clearing a path to deploy troops and vehicles—the fundamental function at which the LAAT-series gunships excel.

REPUBLIC ASSAULT SHIP

THE ARRIVAL OF MASSIVE *ACCLAMATOR*-CLASS TROOPSHIPS above Geonosis is a pivotal moment in galactic military history. The Separatists, working with nefarious corporate organizations, are stunned not only by the decisiveness of the hitherto stagnant Republic, but moreover by its use of a trained and well-equipped clone army—the first time the Republic has deployed an army since its inception. At the battle's turning point, the troopships land to disgorge swarms of armed transport gunships under the cover of turbolaser fire. The ships are accompanied by heavy ground vehicles and thousands of well-trained, dedicated clone troops.

BORN FROM BETRAYAL

The new Galactic Army's arsenal was secretly built by a mighty corporation that could have led the Separatists if not for bloody treachery. Leading Kuati executives were assassinated when Neimoidians took over the Trade Federation at the notorious Eriadu Conference a decade earlier. The outraged industrialists have since aligned with the Supreme Chancellery. Meanwhile, the pace of clandestine construction accelerates in Kuat's cordoned shipyards and factories on Rothana.

Main bridge and battle operations rooms are windowless but furnished with sophisticated holographic displays

Power core cavity is not subject to artificial gravity

Conning tower scanner and communications housing

Assembly hall

Bridge tower module is standard on KDY's smaller naval designs

Power systems maintenance vent

Dorsal turbolaser emplacement

Antigrav repulsorlift generator

Engine servicing release latches

Tensorial integrity field conduits

Power systems cooling neutrino radiator grille

Tail houses extended spinal conduit for inertial compensator fields that maintain integrity of ship's void-filled structure

Thruster particle stream channel

Auxiliary thruster is less powerful than main thruster, but greatly affects turning due to further off-axis location

Smaller lower hangar receives clone troops

Eight electromagnetic thrust-vectoring panels deflect exhaust particle streams to provide turning force

Action-ready gunships drop through hatch facing forward

SUPPORTIVE MOTHERSHIP

Each *Acclamator* coordinates its forces strategically. Orbital bombardments with high-yield proton torpedoes and surgical turbolaser strikes hit enemy fortifications when capture is not a priority. Armies entrenched deep underground may be subject to a last-resort "Base Delta Zero" fleet bombardment. Such operations reduce the upper crust of a planet to molten slag—a spectacle unseen in the Republic until the Clone Wars.

Hyperdrive generator

Antigrav repulsorlifts support most of the ship's weight, but landing pads provide stable ground contact

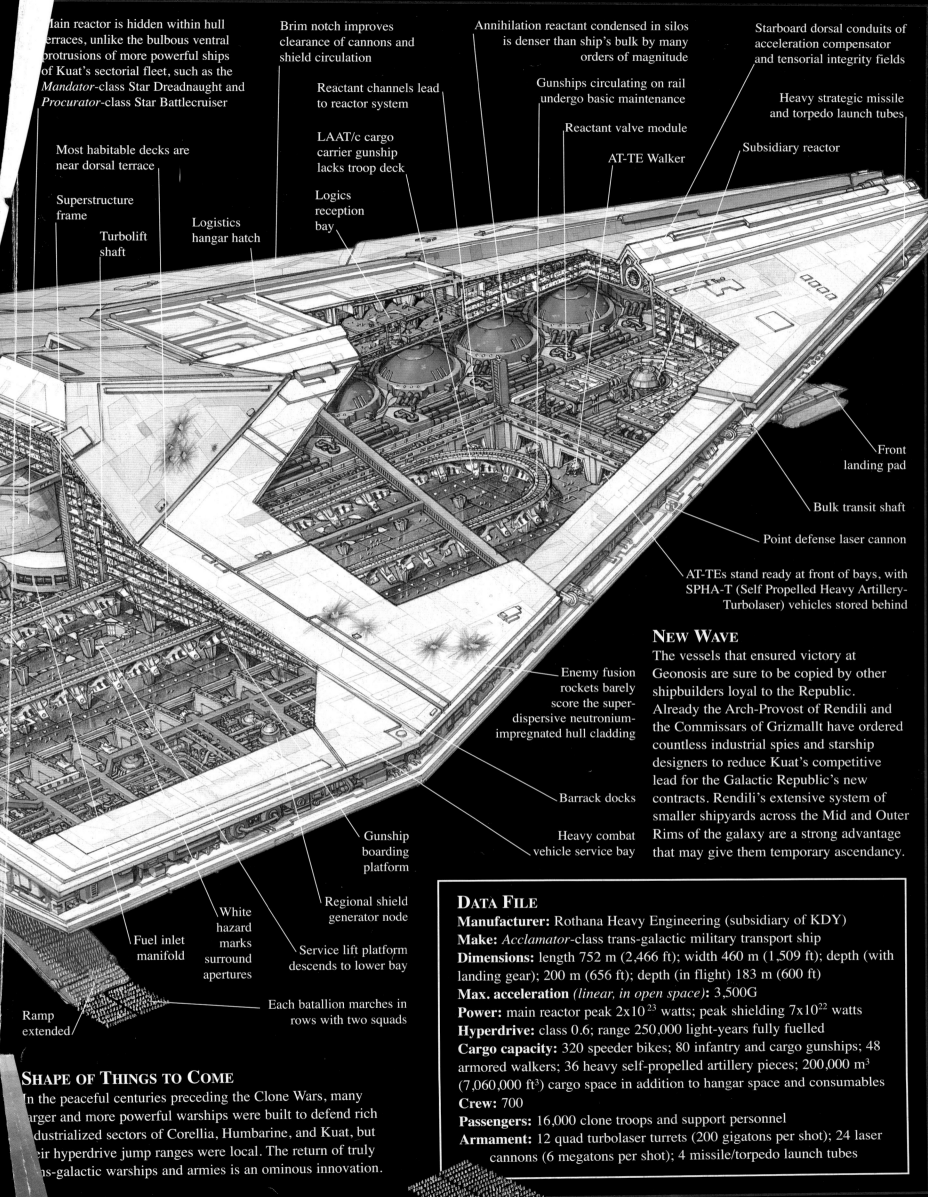

Main reactor is hidden within hull terraces, unlike the bulbous ventral protrusions of more powerful ships of Kuat's sectorial fleet, such as the *Mandator*-class Star Dreadnaught and *Procurator*-class Star Battlecruiser

Brim notch improves clearance of cannons and shield circulation

Annihilation reactant condensed in silos is denser than ship's bulk by many orders of magnitude

Starboard dorsal conduits of acceleration compensator and tensorial integrity fields

Reactant channels lead to reactor system

Gunships circulating on rail undergo basic maintenance

Heavy strategic missile and torpedo launch tubes

Most habitable decks are near dorsal terrace

LAAT/c cargo carrier gunship lacks troop deck

Reactant valve module

Subsidiary reactor

Superstructure frame

Logics reception bay

AT-TE Walker

Turbolift shaft

Logistics hangar hatch

Front landing pad

Bulk transit shaft

Point defense laser cannon

AT-TEs stand ready at front of bays, with SPHA-T (Self Propelled Heavy Artillery-Turbolaser) vehicles stored behind

Enemy fusion rockets barely score the super-dispersive neutronium-impregnated hull cladding

NEW WAVE

The vessels that ensured victory at Geonosis are sure to be copied by other shipbuilders loyal to the Republic. Already the Arch-Provost of Rendili and the Commissars of Grizmallt have ordered countless industrial spies and starship designers to reduce Kuat's competitive lead for the Galactic Republic's new contracts. Rendili's extensive system of smaller shipyards across the Mid and Outer Rims of the galaxy are a strong advantage that may give them temporary ascendancy.

Barrack docks

Heavy combat vehicle service bay

Gunship boarding platform

Regional shield generator node

White hazard marks surround apertures

Service lift platform descends to lower bay

Fuel inlet manifold

Ramp extended

Each batallion marches in rows with two squads

SHAPE OF THINGS TO COME

In the peaceful centuries preceding the Clone Wars, many larger and more powerful warships were built to defend rich industrialized sectors of Corellia, Humbarine, and Kuat, but their hyperdrive jump ranges were local. The return of truly trans-galactic warships and armies is an ominous innovation.

DATA FILE

Manufacturer: Rothana Heavy Engineering (subsidiary of KDY)
Make: *Acclamator*-class trans-galactic military transport ship
Dimensions: length 752 m (2,466 ft); width 460 m (1,509 ft); depth (with landing gear); 200 m (656 ft); depth (in flight) 183 m (600 ft)
Max. acceleration (*linear, in open space*): 3,500G
Power: main reactor peak 2×10^{23} watts; peak shielding 7×10^{22} watts
Hyperdrive: class 0.6; range 250,000 light-years fully fuelled
Cargo capacity: 320 speeder bikes; 80 infantry and cargo gunships; 48 armored walkers; 36 heavy self-propelled artillery pieces; 200,000 m³ (7,060,000 ft³) cargo space in addition to hangar space and consumables
Crew: 700
Passengers: 16,000 clone troops and support personnel
Armament: 12 quad turbolaser turrets (200 gigatons per shot); 24 laser cannons (6 megatons per shot); 4 missile/torpedo launch tubes

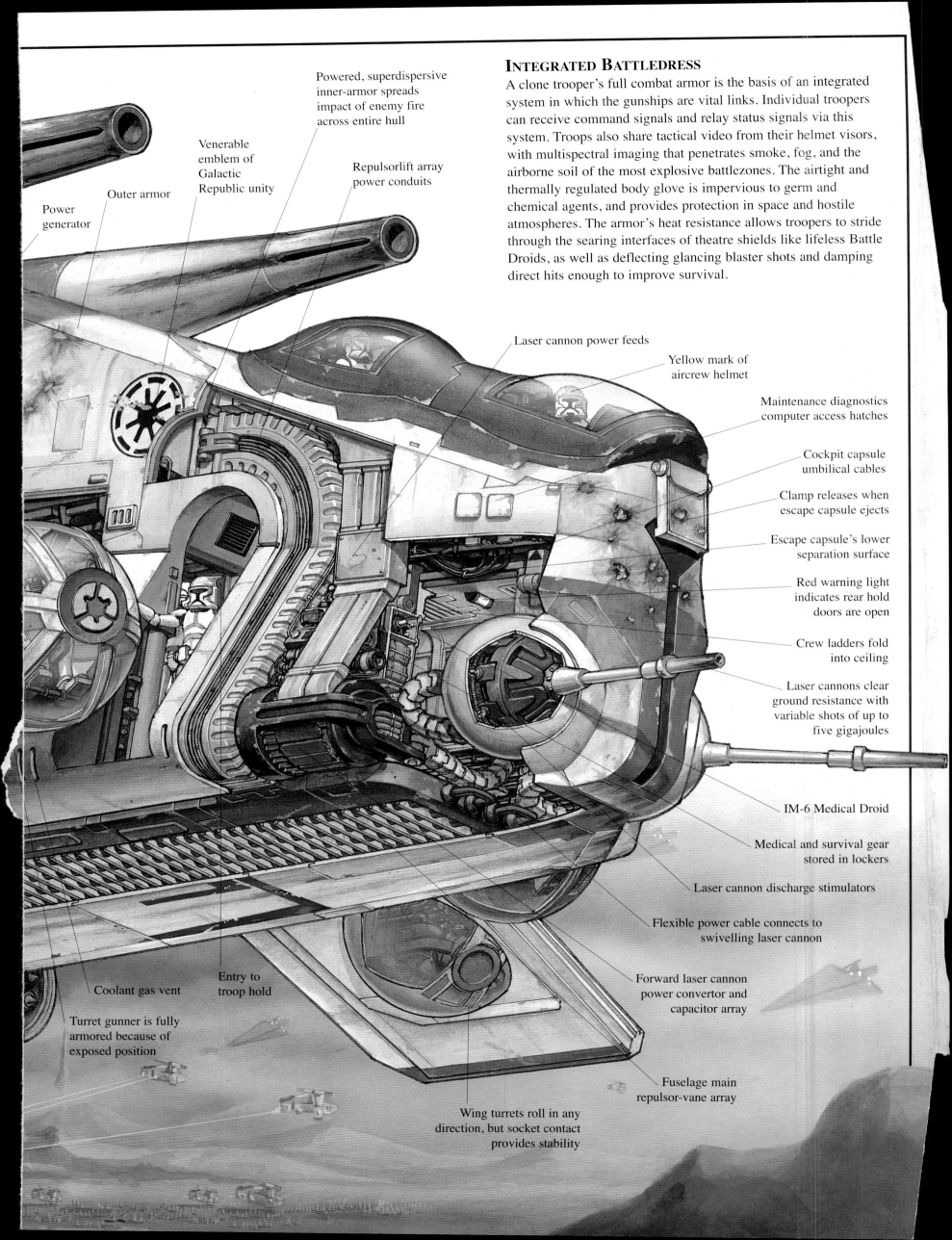

Power
generator

Outer armor

Venerable
emblem of
Galactic
Republic unity

Powered, superdispersive
inner-armor spreads
impact of enemy fire
across entire hull

Repulsorlift array
power conduits

INTEGRATED BATTLEDRESS

A clone trooper's full combat armor is the basis of an integrated system in which the gunships are vital links. Individual troopers can receive command signals and relay status signals via this system. Troops also share tactical video from their helmet visors, with multispectral imaging that penetrates smoke, fog, and the airborne soil of the most explosive battlezones. The airtight and thermally regulated body glove is impervious to germ and chemical agents, and provides protection in space and hostile atmospheres. The armor's heat resistance allows troopers to stride through the searing interfaces of theatre shields like lifeless Battle Droids, as well as deflecting glancing blaster shots and damping direct hits enough to improve survival.

Laser cannon power feeds

Yellow mark of
aircrew helmet

Maintenance diagnostics
computer access hatches

Cockpit capsule
umbilical cables

Clamp releases when
escape capsule ejects

Escape capsule's lower
separation surface

Red warning light
indicates rear hold
doors are open

Crew ladders fold
into ceiling

Laser cannons clear
ground resistance with
variable shots of up to
five gigajoules

IM-6 Medical Droid

Medical and survival gear
stored in lockers

Laser cannon discharge stimulators

Flexible power cable connects to
swivelling laser cannon

Forward laser cannon
power convertor and
capacitor array

Fuselage main
repulsor-vane array

Wing turrets roll in any
direction, but socket contact
provides stability

Entry to
troop hold

Coolant gas vent

Turret gunner is fully
armored because of
exposed position

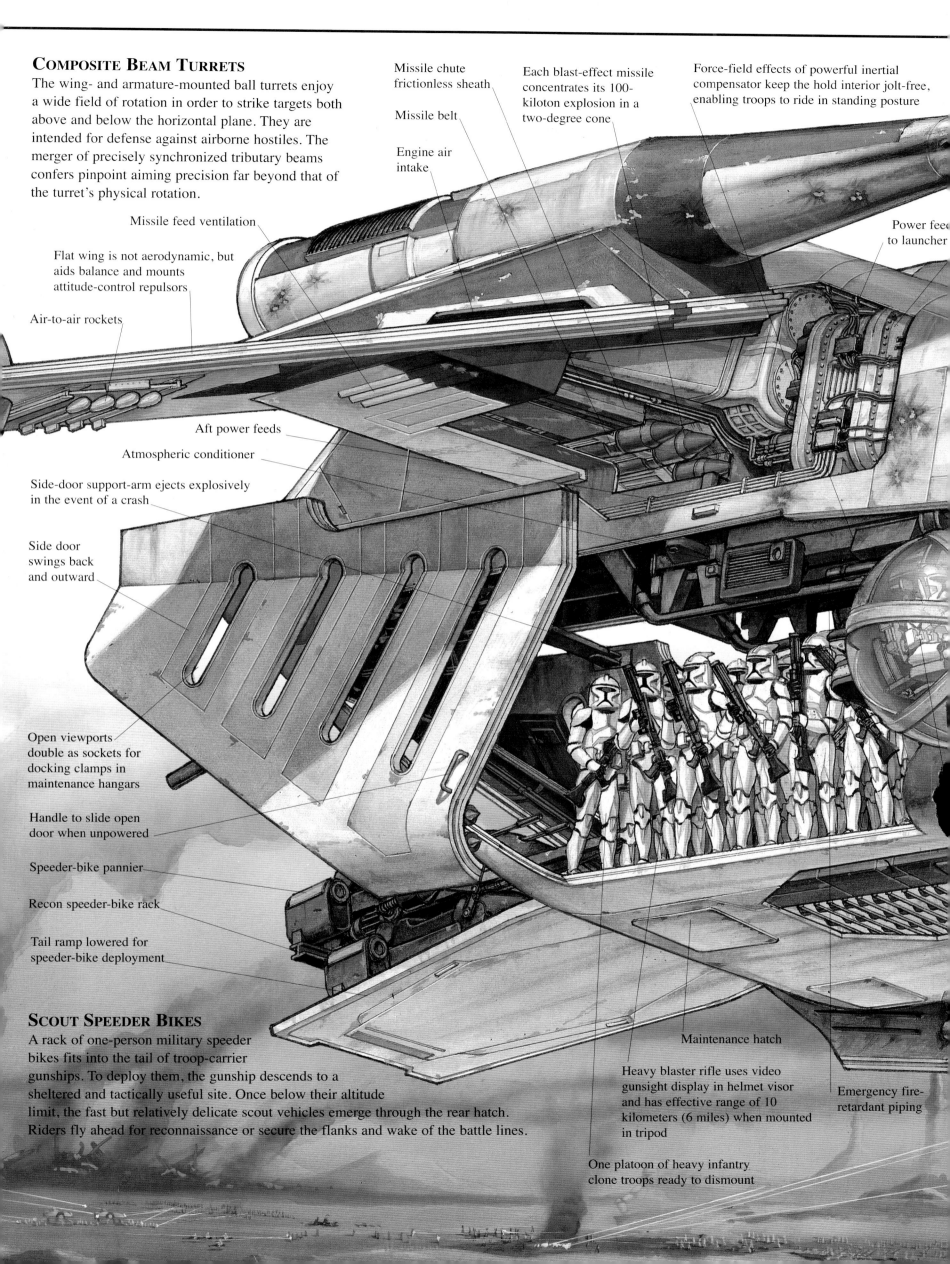

COMPOSITE BEAM TURRETS

The wing- and armature-mounted ball turrets enjoy a wide field of rotation in order to strike targets both above and below the horizontal plane. They are intended for defense against airborne hostiles. The merger of precisely synchronized tributary beams confers pinpoint aiming precision far beyond that of the turret's physical rotation.

Missile feed ventilation

Flat wing is not aerodynamic, but aids balance and mounts attitude-control repulsors

Air-to-air rockets

Aft power feeds

Atmospheric conditioner

Side-door support-arm ejects explosively in the event of a crash

Side door swings back and outward

Open viewports double as sockets for docking clamps in maintenance hangars

Handle to slide open door when unpowered

Speeder-bike pannier

Recon speeder-bike rack

Tail ramp lowered for speeder-bike deployment

Missile chute frictionless sheath

Missile belt

Engine air intake

Each blast-effect missile concentrates its 100-kiloton explosion in a two-degree cone

Force-field effects of powerful inertial compensator keep the hold interior jolt-free, enabling troops to ride in standing posture

Power feed to launcher

SCOUT SPEEDER BIKES

A rack of one-person military speeder bikes fits into the tail of troop-carrier gunships. To deploy them, the gunship descends to a sheltered and tactically useful site. Once below their altitude limit, the fast but relatively delicate scout vehicles emerge through the rear hatch. Riders fly ahead for reconnaissance or secure the flanks and wake of the battle lines.

Maintenance hatch

Heavy blaster rifle uses video gunsight display in helmet visor and has effective range of 10 kilometers (6 miles) when mounted in tripod

Emergency fire-retardant piping

One platoon of heavy infantry clone troops ready to dismount

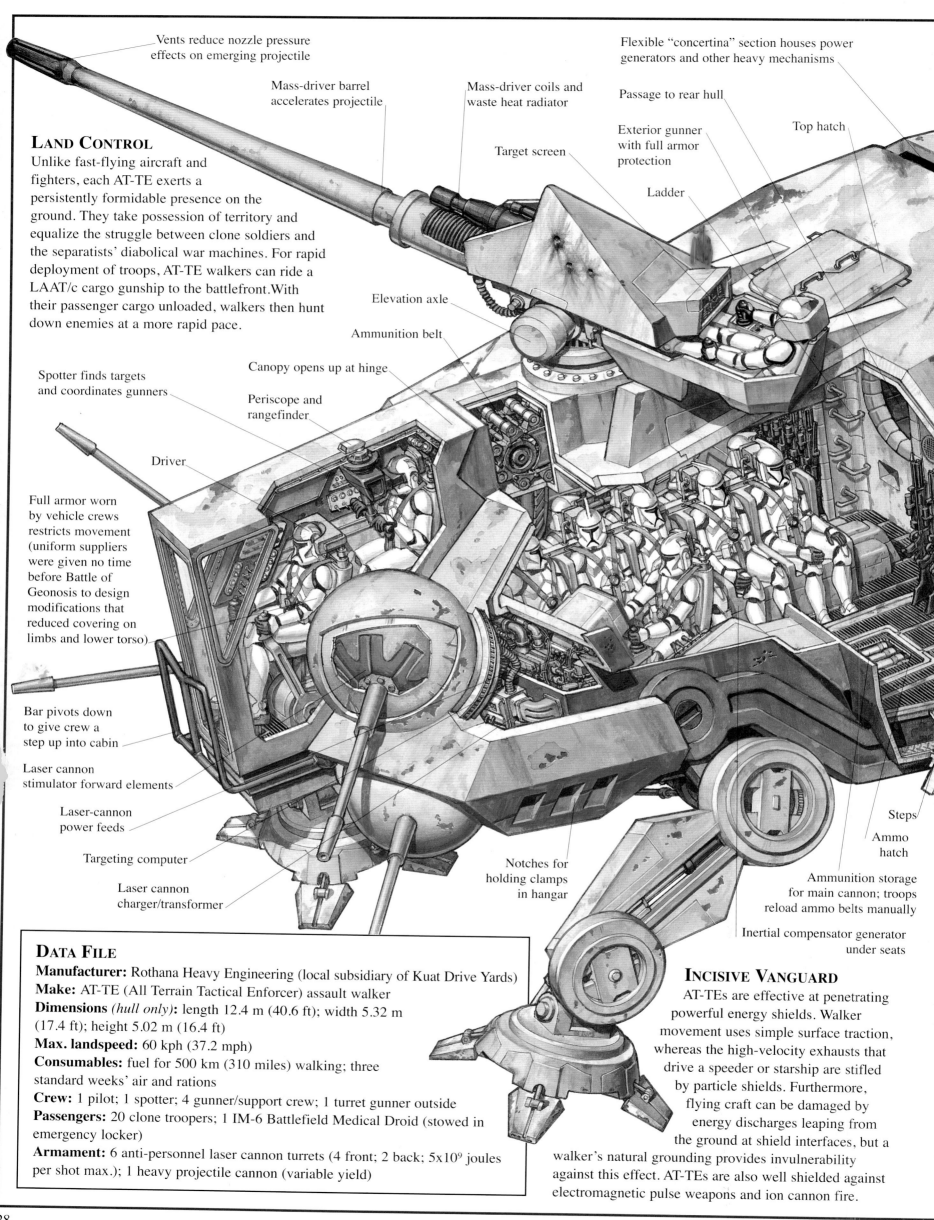

Vents reduce nozzle pressure effects on emerging projectile

Mass-driver barrel accelerates projectile

Mass-driver coils and waste heat radiator

Target screen

Flexible "concertina" section houses power generators and other heavy mechanisms

Passage to rear hull

Exterior gunner with full armor protection

Top hatch

Ladder

LAND CONTROL

Unlike fast-flying aircraft and fighters, each AT-TE exerts a persistently formidable presence on the ground. They take possession of territory and equalize the struggle between clone soldiers and the separatists' diabolical war machines. For rapid deployment of troops, AT-TE walkers can ride a LAAT/c cargo gunship to the battlefront. With their passenger cargo unloaded, walkers then hunt down enemies at a more rapid pace.

Elevation axle

Ammunition belt

Canopy opens up at hinge

Spotter finds targets and coordinates gunners

Periscope and rangefinder

Driver

Full armor worn by vehicle crews restricts movement (uniform suppliers were given no time before Battle of Geonosis to design modifications that reduced covering on limbs and lower torso)

Bar pivots down to give crew a step up into cabin

Laser cannon stimulator forward elements

Laser-cannon power feeds

Targeting computer

Laser cannon charger/transformer

Notches for holding clamps in hangar

Steps

Ammo hatch

Ammunition storage for main cannon; troops reload ammo belts manually

Inertial compensator generator under seats

DATA FILE

Manufacturer: Rothana Heavy Engineering (local subsidiary of Kuat Drive Yards)
Make: AT-TE (All Terrain Tactical Enforcer) assault walker
Dimensions *(hull only)*: length 12.4 m (40.6 ft); width 5.32 m (17.4 ft); height 5.02 m (16.4 ft)
Max. landspeed: 60 kph (37.2 mph)
Consumables: fuel for 500 km (310 miles) walking; three standard weeks' air and rations
Crew: 1 pilot; 1 spotter; 4 gunner/support crew; 1 turret gunner outside
Passengers: 20 clone troopers; 1 IM-6 Battlefield Medical Droid (stowed in emergency locker)
Armament: 6 anti-personnel laser cannon turrets (4 front; 2 back; 5×10^9 joules per shot max.); 1 heavy projectile cannon (variable yield)

INCISIVE VANGUARD

AT-TEs are effective at penetrating powerful energy shields. Walker movement uses simple surface traction, whereas the high-velocity exhausts that drive a speeder or starship are stifled by particle shields. Furthermore, flying craft can be damaged by energy discharges leaping from the ground at shield interfaces, but a walker's natural grounding provides invulnerability against this effect. AT-TEs are also well shielded against electromagnetic pulse weapons and ion cannon fire.

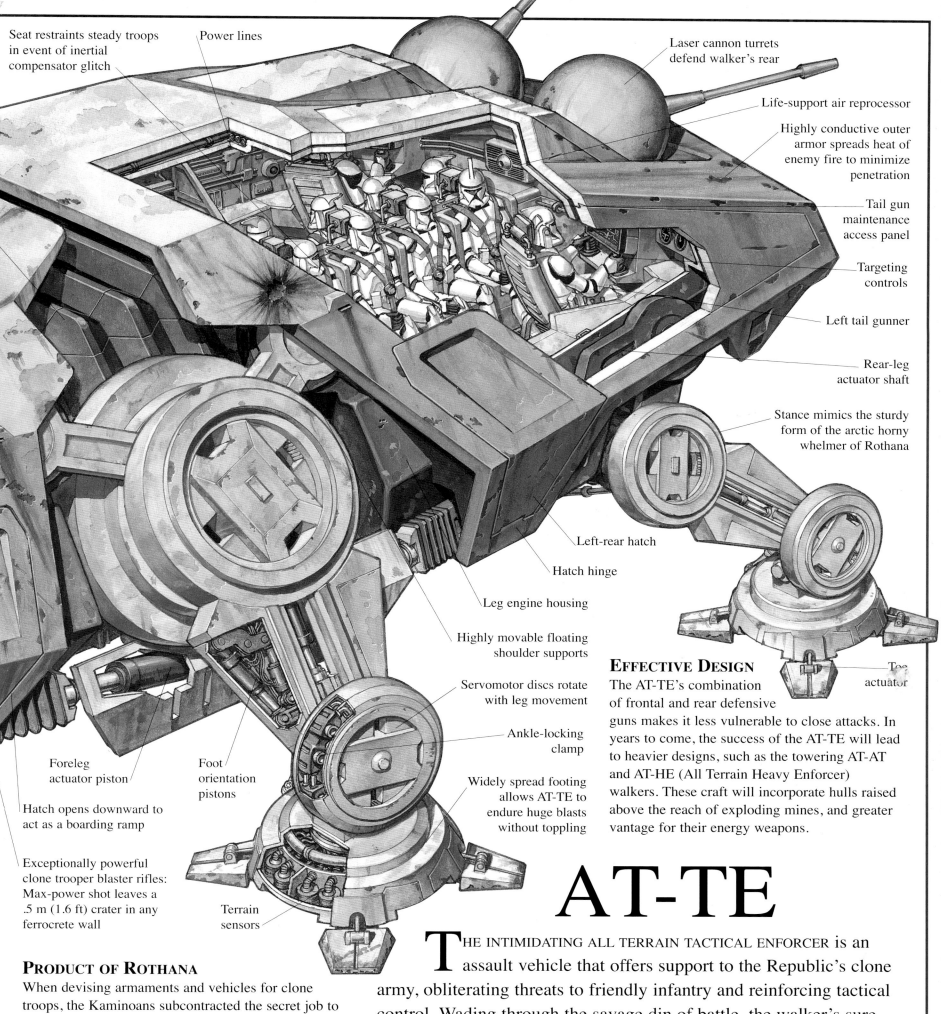

Seat restraints steady troops in event of inertial compensator glitch

Power lines

Laser cannon turrets defend walker's rear

Life-support air reprocessor

Highly conductive outer armor spreads heat of enemy fire to minimize penetration

Tail gun maintenance access panel

Targeting controls

Left tail gunner

Rear-leg actuator shaft

Stance mimics the sturdy form of the arctic horny whelmer of Rothana

Left-rear hatch

Hatch hinge

Leg engine housing

Highly movable floating shoulder supports

Servomotor discs rotate with leg movement

Ankle-locking clamp

Widely spread footing allows AT-TE to endure huge blasts without toppling

Foreleg actuator piston

Foot orientation pistons

Hatch opens downward to act as a boarding ramp

Exceptionally powerful clone trooper blaster rifles: Max-power shot leaves a .5 m (1.6 ft) crater in any ferrocrete wall

Terrain sensors

Toe actuator

EFFECTIVE DESIGN

The AT-TE's combination of frontal and rear defensive guns makes it less vulnerable to close attacks. In years to come, the success of the AT-TE will lead to heavier designs, such as the towering AT-AT and AT-HE (All Terrain Heavy Enforcer) walkers. These craft will incorporate hulls raised above the reach of exploding mines, and greater vantage for their energy weapons.

AT-TE

THE INTIMIDATING ALL TERRAIN TACTICAL ENFORCER is an assault vehicle that offers support to the Republic's clone army, obliterating threats to friendly infantry and reinforcing tactical control. Wading through the savage din of battle, the walker's sure-footed, six-legged stance allows it to cross crevices and climb otherwise impassably rugged slopes. Its massive turret-mounted missile-launcher bombards fixed emplacements or smites slow-moving aircraft, while six laser-cannon turrets swivel quickly to devastate faster line-of-sight targets. In the event of a close assault by enemy infantry, an AT-TE can dismount its two squads of troops to enter the fray and secure the immediate surroundings.

PRODUCT OF ROTHANA

When devising armaments and vehicles for clone troops, the Kaminoans subcontracted the secret job to Rothana Heavy Engineering, a subsidiary of Kuat Drive Yards—and no friend of the Trade Federation or Techno Union. Toiling in immense underground factories and honeycombed orbital shipyards, RHE's workforce is famed for their diligence. Their star system is uniquely clear of Trade Federation espionage, due to factors ranging from the impenetrably complex Rothanian etiquette (which makes outsiders stand out) to a sizeable KDY corporate-security starfleet and inventively deployed mines in Rothana's inbound hyperlanes.

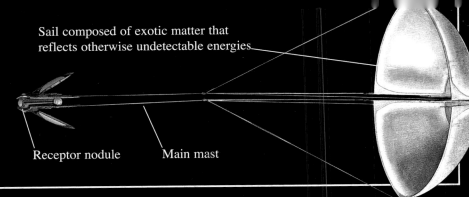

SAIL POWER

The delicate reflector-surfaces of most "solar" sails unfurl to moon-like diameters, and are more commonly pushed by tachyon streams and ultraviolet lasers than sunlight. Dooku's unique sail, however, achieves similar performance across the entire galaxy with a much smaller span and no detectable support system. This unexplained mobility enhances Dooku's commanding mystique in Geonosian eyes.

Sail composed of exotic matter that reflects otherwise undetectable energies

Receptor nodule

Main mast

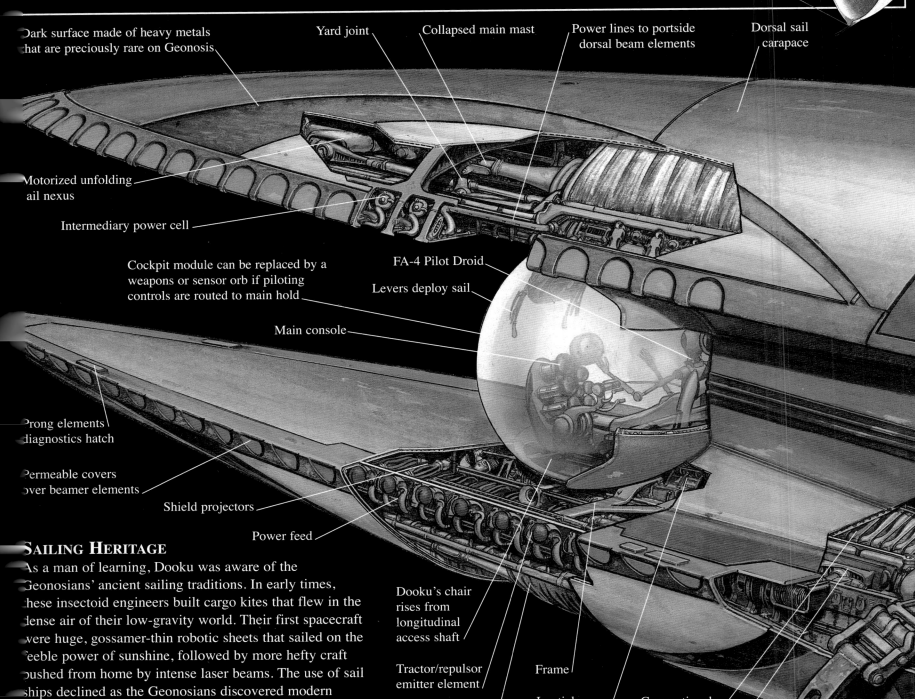

Dark surface made of heavy metals that are preciously rare on Geonosis

Yard joint

Collapsed main mast

Power lines to portside dorsal beam elements

Dorsal sail carapace

Motorized unfolding sail nexus

Intermediary power cell

Cockpit module can be replaced by a weapons or sensor orb if piloting controls are routed to main hold

FA-4 Pilot Droid

Levers deploy sail

Main console

Prong elements diagnostics hatch

Permeable covers over beamer elements

Shield projectors

Power feed

Dooku's chair rises from longitudinal access shaft

Tractor/repulsor emitter element

Furled ventral sail

Frame

Inertial compensator

Conventional scanner array

Repulsorlift generator

Landing-gear actuators

Last segment is jointed to spread ship's weight

SAILING HERITAGE

As a man of learning, Dooku was aware of the Geonosians' ancient sailing traditions. In early times, these insectoid engineers built cargo kites that flew in the dense air of their low-gravity world. Their first spacecraft were huge, gossamer-thin robotic sheets that sailed on the feeble power of sunshine, followed by more hefty craft pushed from home by intense laser beams. The use of sail ships declined as the Geonosians discovered modern fusion technologies—although Poggle the Lesser, Archduke of Geonosis, was pleased to draw on ancient technology in order to accommodate an esteemed ally.

DATA FILE

Manufacturer: Huppla Pasa Tisc Shipwrights Collective
Make: *Punworcca 116*-class interstellar sloop
Dimensions: length 15.2 m (49.8 ft); width 4.6m (15 ft); depth 4.8m (15.7 ft)
Max. acceleration: sail approx. 1,000G; thrusters 30G
Max. airspeed: 1,600 kph (992 mph)
Crew: 1 droid pilot; optional living co-pilot
Passengers: 1 in cabin; standing room for 10
Hyperdrive : class 1.5
Armament: 84 narrow tractor/repulsor beams

MYSTERIOUS ANTIQUE

After leaving the Jedi Order, Dooku began to develop a taste for rare, pre-Republic artifacts. An antiques dealer near the Gree Enclave sold him an ancient sail, which demonstrates unique and startling properties. The sail is powered by an as-yet undetectable source of supralight emissions, allowing Dooku's custom ship an independence, and style, unknown by any other current space-faring vehicle

SOLAR SAILER

Aᴀ GIFT FROM HIS GEONOSIAN COLLEAGUES, Dooku's ship is a unique melding of a *Punworcca 116*-class sloop with an elegant sail supplied by the Count himself. On Dooku's instructions, Geonosian engineers attached this enigmatic accessory to the ship to provide independent power without the need to carry fuel (apart from guide thrusters). The ship's interior is tailored to Dooku's sense of refinement, with an extensive databook library and ornate decorations. When the tide of battle turns, the Count flees to his escape vessel and slips away....

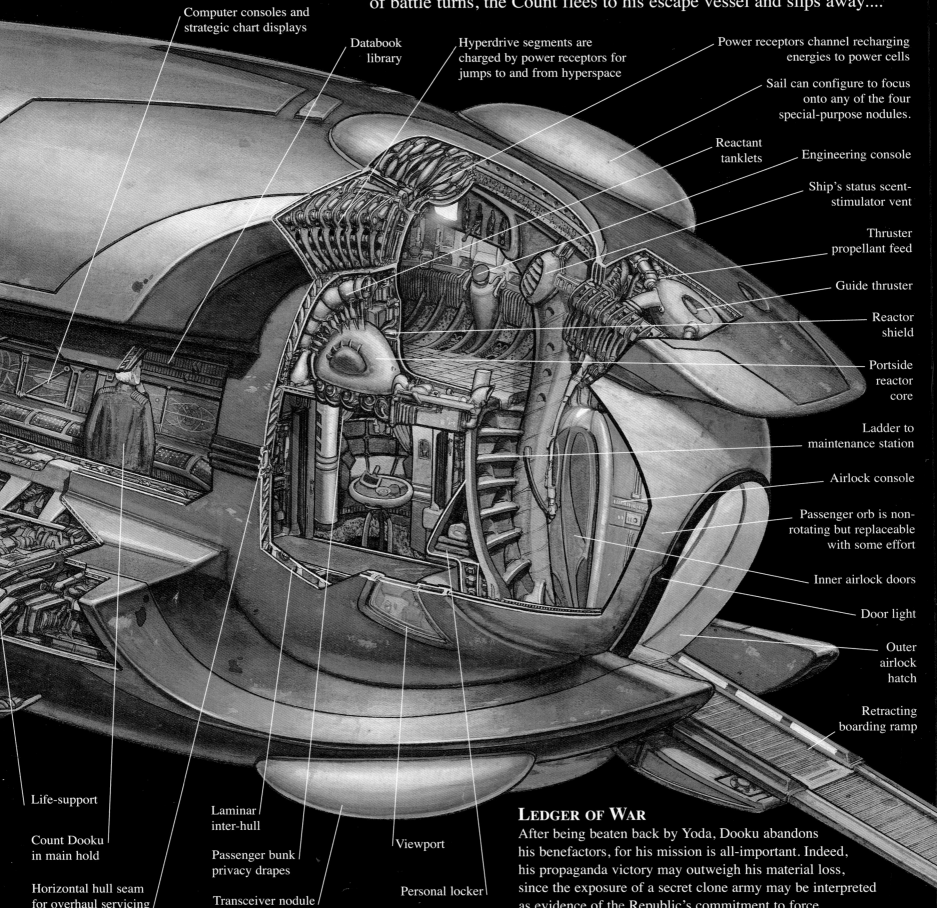

BOW PRONGS
Geonosian starships typically feature two or more multi-functional bow prongs. Rows of narrow-beam tractor/repulsor emitters along the prongs act as offensive grapples or steering aids when there are surrounding objects to pull and push against. Also, the spread of ray-shield energies around the prongs can be selectively adjusted to give the ship extra maneuverablity.

Computer consoles and strategic chart displays

Databook library

Hyperdrive segments are charged by power receptors for jumps to and from hyperspace

Power receptors channel recharging energies to power cells

Sail can configure to focus onto any of the four special-purpose nodules.

Reactant tanklets

Engineering console

Ship's status scent-stimulator vent

Thruster propellant feed

Guide thruster

Reactor shield

Portside reactor core

Ladder to maintenance station

Airlock console

Passenger orb is non-rotating but replaceable with some effort

Inner airlock doors

Door light

Outer airlock hatch

Retracting boarding ramp

Life-support

Count Dooku in main hold

Horizontal hull seam for overhaul servicing

Laminar inter-hull

Passenger bunk privacy drapes

Transceiver nodule

Viewport

Personal locker

LEDGER OF WAR
After being beaten back by Yoda, Dooku abandons his benefactors, for his mission is all-important. Indeed, his propaganda victory may outweigh his material loss, since the exposure of a secret clone army may be interpreted as evidence of the Republic's commitment to force.

First American edition, 2002

2 4 6 8 10 9 7 5 3 1

Published in the United States by DK Publishing, Inc.
95 Madison Avenue, New York, New York 10016

Published in Great Britain by Dorling Kindersley Limited.

ISBN 0-7894-8574-5

A catalog record is available from the Library of Congress

Colour reproduction by Dot Reprographics, England
Printed and bound in Italy by A. Mondadori Editore, Verona

ACKNOWLEDGEMENTS

HANS JENSSEN painted the Naboo Cruiser, Jedi Starfighter, Owen Lars'
Swoop Bike, Republic Assault Ship, Republic Gunship, AT-TE.
He would like to thank: Janine Morris for her support in looking after
Arne, cooking meals, and putting up with bad moods; Doug Chiang for the
ride in his Porsche. He would like to dedicate his contribution to the memory
of his friend, Laura Griffiths.

RICHARD CHASEMORE painted Zam's Airspeeder, Anakin's Airspeeder, *Slave I*,
Padmé's Starship, Trade Federation Core Ship, Geonosian Fighter, Solar Sailer.
He would like to thank: Hilary Craig, for being fantastic; everyone at Skywalker
Ranch, for making us so welcome, especially Doug Chiang, the source of endless
inspiration; and the guys at Superglider, for their inspirational music.

The illustrators would also like to thank: Fay David and all at the Art Department; the
animatics guys, for being incredibly welcoming and generous with their time;
particular mention must go to Robert Kinkead, who worked up several of the angles
for us; and Simon and BJ, for letting us win one game of table football in two weeks
of trying! Also, of course, our friend Iain Morris for all his help.

CURTIS SAXTON would like to thank the following people:
Simon Beecroft, who has been a peerless organizer,
a champion of reason, and savior of much that is
indispensable in this book; John Kelly, who upheld
and perfected the widest and deepest visions of our
project, even in the face of structural changes and
challenges that initially daunted the author; Iain
R. Morris, Chris Cerasi, Leland Chee, Sue
Rostoni, and Jonathan W. Rinzler, who were ever-
helpful gatekeepers and wardens of the evolving
literature, fastidiously ensuring that our
work was reconciled with every "certain
point of view" of any importance; I salute
my collaborators, the artists Richard

Chasemore and Hans Jenssen, for their professionalism, ingenuity, and stoical
fulfilment of "impossible" objectives; Lucy Autrey Wilson, Lucas Licensing, and
Dorling Kindersley, to whom I owe the privilege of official involvement in the *Star
Wars* endeavor; Doug Chiang, who, in our project's most productive brainstorming
session, lent us his valuable time and authoritative insight, saving us weeks of
stumbling in the dark; Dr. David West Reynolds, who offered crucial advocacy,
valued peer feedback and perspective, and a most formidable precedent; above all
others, George Lucas, for the majesty of his grandiose creation and for graciously
permitting the growth of participatory fandom.

I would also like to thank: Pete Briggs, Robert B.K. Brown, Elwyn Chow, Albert
Forge, Adam Gehrls, Martyn Griffiths, Frank Gerratana, Michael Horne, Ethan
Platten, Wayne Poe, Andrew Tse, Anthony Tully, Michael Wong, and Brian Young,
who were prominent among the hundreds of people contributing to constructive
debates about *Star Wars* technicalities over the years, resulting in the consensus of
conceptual and physical foundations applied in these pages; the profuse and
unstinting generosity of Scott Chitwood, Joshua Griffin, their staff and community,
for providing visibility and years of continuity for my private hobby, and special
thanks to Paul Ens for the introduction; Gwendoline Blanchet and the Blanchet
family, Andrew Tse, Nicolas Gruel, Pete Briggs, Kate Wood, and Michael Horne, who
provided encouragement, support, and hospitality on the practical and inspirational
journeys I undertook; my scientific mentors and seniors, Dr. Kinwah Wu,
Dr. Geoff Bicknell, and Dr. Ralph Sutherland, for their wisdom and the experience
of methodical investigation, and for a career concerning the wonders of the real
universe; finally, I thank Tyler Saxton for helping to set my course when he
lent me the use of his Vidi Amiga video digitizer for my first *Star Wars*
investigations so many years ago.

DORLING KINDERSLEY would like to thank Julia March,
for invaluable editorial assistance; Chris Gollaher
and Steve Chianesi, for helping with continuity
issues; Paul Ens and Pablo Hidalgo, for online
support; Aaron Henderson, for fulfilling our
never-ending image requests.

www.starwars.com
www.starwarskids.com

copyright © 2002 Lucasfilm Ltd. & ™ .

See our complete
catalog at
www.dk.com